I QUIT!

I QUIT!

THE 50 WORST JOBS IN BRITAIN
BY TIM WILD

First published in 2004 by

Virgin Books
Thames Wharf Studios
Rainville Rd
London W6 9HA

Text copyright © Tim Wild
Interior photographs copyright © Kerri Sharp

ISBN 0 7535 0986 5

Design and typesetting by Smith & Gilmour, London
Printed and bound by Mackays of Chatham plc, Chatham, Kent

For Kirsten

Author biography

Author Tim Wild has had several tempestuous run-ins with paid employment. Thankfully none of them has left any permanent scars. To make ends meet, he occasionally allows magazines to pay him for writing things down. When not watching the TV, playing computer games, doing the *Guardian* crossword, eating delicious food and flying kites, he likes to relax with friends. This is his first book.

Acknowledgements

Special thanks to all who made this book possible: Ewen MacIntosh and Rhian Evans at Form Talent, editor and photographer Kerri Sharp, all at Smith & Gilmour, my mum and dad, Kirsten, Richard Wild, Nick Friedman, Hannah Lamb, James Marriott, Andrew Mueller, Andrew Collins, Peter Paphides, John Warr, Ciaran Walsh, Greg Jarvis, Thomas H Green, Alison Dodd, Nick Bateman, Adam Hollier, Mike Slocombe, Gary Bleasdale, Arthur Lager, Rebecca Levene, Andy 'Lord' Lockett and Laurence Howell.

CONTENTS

Foreword by Ewen MacIntosh –

'Keith' from the multiple-award-winning BBC comedy series *The Office*

Congratulations! You are now in possession of the only essential guide to the 50 worst jobs in Britain you will ever need. If you're standing in the bookshop killing time and have no intention of buying this marvellous volume, then I hope fate takes its revenge and you spend the rest of your days roaming the sewers dressed as a chicken-plucking banana. The rest of you lovely people can relax in the knowledge that you will never suffer the indignities described in the following pages, or, if you do, you will have the perfect primer to see you through. It's inevitable that, in the course of a lifetime, the jobs we have shape us in all sorts of ways. People meet their future spouses through work, make lifelong friends, have experiences that will stay with them for ever and achieve genuine fulfilment and happiness. Of course, occasionally you turn up for a job and find out you're going to be knee-deep in shit for thirteen hours a day. Such is life.

I came to be involved in this book through a job. Tim Wild and I were both writing for a music magazine in late 2003. (A magazine, incidentally, whose publishers decided to shut down two and a half weeks before Christmas and sack all the staff. How's that for a job that turns round and bites you on the ass?) When he came to write this book he thought of me: not for my unique and boisterous writing style – that's just a bonus – but because of another job I had.

I remember very clearly the day my agent called me up and asked if I wanted to spend six weeks 'working in the office'. I couldn't believe it had come to this. Things were going so badly that I was being offered temp work at the agency premises just to tide me over. But no, she was of course referring to the BBC sitcom that would change my life and, up until now, keep me away from those jobs that are little more than ritualised daily abuses.

A lot of people aren't able to watch *The Office*, or, if they are, then it's through their fingers, wincing and squirming as they see their own working environment uncannily reflected on screen. Being employed in the offices of a paper merchant is not a traditional 'bad job', but the tedium and monotony, combined with the hellish familiarity of one's co-workers' habits, is something that many people recognise and relate to. The scene I receive most comments about involves my character, Keith, getting his annual appraisal from boss David Brent. Something in this scene struck a chord with viewers, particularly those who have been subjected to similar scrutiny from their bosses and their 'where do you see yourself in five years?' interrogations. The truth is we had to film the scene so many times due to Ricky Gervais's constant horseplay, so what you see on screen is a strange combination of genuine frustration and a desperate attempt to get through the next take without laughing. Somehow the scene worked – a testament to brilliant editing if ever there was one. All in all, the series was great to work on, and I'm sure I wasn't the only cast member to wish that every role could be like that.

I've been lucky in that I've had only one job in my life that I truly, truly hated and considered to be a habitual humiliation rather than employment. It was my first-ever job. Living in an army town while I was at school, I found myself one summer in the unfortunate position of 'Cleaner of the Sergeants' Mess'. They didn't dress it up in those days, so I wasn't even allowed the morsel of self-respect I might have recovered had I been titled 'Hygiene Delivery Officer' or 'Dirtlessness Provider'. No sirree, Bob – I was a cleaner, and that was all there was to it. Cleaning is a hound of a job at the best of times. It's Sisyphean; you are effectively in hell. And anyone who considers cleaning to be therapeutic has never had to deal with the detritus left behind by beer-swilling, curry-guzzling, lust-deprived soldiers. It's not pretty, believe me. These guys seemed to be partying every night and I had to come in every morning and literally clean up their mess.

One of the happiest days of my life occurred after I'd been there two weeks, came in one morning and saw that some girl was already taking my mop, bucket and cornucopia of cleaning aids out of the cupboard. What was going on? 'Oh . . . er . . . Debbie wants to have a word with you,' was the only reply. Debbie was what nowadays would be called my 'line manager', but back then was just known as 'the bitch'. I marched towards her office, my face hot with the embarrassment of everyone else clearly knowing I had been fired before I knew myself. It's hard to ask for a second chance when your replacement is already busy getting on with your job. I could already tell that the new girl was better than me: she'd been in five minutes and already had her marigolds on – a task that usually took me a good ten minutes to achieve. And I bet she didn't even have to use her teeth, the clever cow. So I accepted defeat; took it on the chin. I'd finished my first job and, touch wood, my worst job. And I'd survived. As I strolled away from the Mess, I felt a surge of happiness that was entirely new to me. I'd discovered the best thing about having to do an awful job: the moment you leave it. In my case, the moment involved being fired, but in plenty of other cases up and down the country, maybe even in your case, it's the time for you to say, 'I quit!'

WHO FIRST INVENTED WORK, AND BOUND THE FREE AND HOLIDAY-REJOICING SPIRIT DOWN TO THAT DRY DRUDGERY AT THE DESK'S DEAD WOOD? SABBATHLESS SATAN!

CHARLES LAMB

I Quit!

Exactly. Whoever came up with the idea of work deserves a solid kicking. Modern society would have you believe that work is the new religion, that you are what you do. The search for fulfilment from one's day-to-day employment has become the all-consuming passion of the modern age, with those lacking a profession left believing they have little purpose in life. Now, it's all well and good to bang on about the financial rewards and emotional satisfaction that work can bring, but those who most often spread the good news of the Protestant work ethic are those for whom work is on the whole a pleasant affair: nice office, good hours, efficient water coolers and a slinky computer. Try telling someone who spends a goodly amount of their waking hours rummaging through other people's effluent that work is spiritually rewarding and see how far it gets you.

Most of us will have had to endure a terrible job at some point in our lives. Something that was so dull, smelly, dangerous or soul-sappingly pointless that we can still remember it years afterwards. This may have been a Saturday job stacking shelves, a student bar job pulling pints or waiting tables, or maybe you're still doing one right now. This book isn't meant to demean those who are trapped in such a position or clinging on by their financial fingernails doing something that they hate. Instead, it's a sideways look at the world of work and some of the more extreme and ridiculous ways to make a living that British employers have managed to come up with.

Alongside the ruthlessly researched entries, there are a number of more personal tales from luminaries such as writer and broadcaster Andrew Collins, journalist and author Andrew Mueller, journalist Peter Paphides and others. So plaster on a fake smile, put on your industrial rubber gloves and get stuck in to the 50 worst jobs in Britain.

CHAPTER ONE

FACING THE PUBLIC

THERE IS NOT A MORE MEAN, STUPID, DASTARDLY, PITIFUL, SELFISH, SPITEFUL, ENVIOUS, UNGRATEFUL ANIMAL THAN THE PUBLIC. IT IS THE GREATEST OF COWARDS, FOR IT IS AFRAID OF ITSELF. WILLIAM HAZLITT

I Quit!

This quote might have been written by one of Britain's greatest essayists, but anyone who has walked down Oxford Street on a Saturday lunchtime will have probably thought something similar. There is something about seeing human behaviour en masse that gets our goat, brings out the individual and the rebel from within us, and sets us on edge. And there is an ironic paradox here: even though collectively we are all part of that mass, we prefer to think of ourselves as distanced observers – individuals with refined aesthetic tastes and ambitions. We are never 'them' – the general public – who dawdle on the pavement at inappropriate moments, look gormless in the face of rational answers to their dumb questions and, sometimes, display the ugly side of human behaviour.

Unfortunately, the nature of some people's jobs means there is no escape from the general public. These workers are on the front line of face-to-face contact with an unknown quantity and at the mercy of the mob. Whether this involves working behind a counter in a frantically busy sandwich bar or herding the pastel-clad hordes onto a theme-park ride, anyone who has had the experience of facing 'them' on a day-to-day basis will have been astounded by their lack of common courtesy, common sense and basic hygiene. Not for nothing are they called the great unwashed. Perhaps there's another chapter to be written about the delightful qualities of our fellow man, where old people are helped across the street and pushchairs carried up the escalator and where helpful staff are thanked by grateful customers. But this isn't it. Here we look at the jobs where the public are out in force, consuming at large and taking no prisoners.

Outdoor Promotions Operative

UNOFFICIAL JOB TITLE >> Human Signpost

WAGES >> something paltry per hour

HOURS >> 9a.m. – 5p.m. Monday to Saturday

LOCATION >> Oxford Street, London, right in everyone else's way

UNIFORM >> Hat, coat, scarf, gloves, shades and protective menacing glare

SPECIALIST SKILLS >> Two feet, at least one working hand and a Teflon-like resistance to boredom

I quit!

There aren't many jobs in the world where you can be safe in the knowledge that, if the laws on street advertising in London were to change, you'd instantly be replaced by a barrel of cement with a stick in it. The unstoppable flow of technical progress has always been a mixed blessing for the humble worker, particularly those in an industrial capacity. As technology develops which makes jobs easier, faster and cheaper to carry out, workers often find themselves both literally and figuratively redundant when they are replaced by machines who can work longer hours, require no pay and don't sneak off to the toilets for a fag every ten minutes.

The word 'saboteur' originates from a group of French workers who, angry at the technology that threatened to replace them, threw their heavy wooden sandals (called sabots) into the new-fangled gizmos and broke them. A Gallic breed similar to the Luddite, one assumes. However, in this fast-paced digital age, there's a certain amount of perverse comfort in the fact that there's still a job out there that no machine could ever replace: standing in the street holding a bit of wood. That's right, just standing there, holding a sign. Normally it will be advertising a 'golf sale', an event so special that they have it every day of the week. How many serious golfers shop in Oxford Street on a busy Saturday anyway?

This job isn't particularly difficult – it requires no specialist skills or qualifications apart from being able to stand upright and hold on to a stick. The truly inventive ones stuff the stick into a rucksack, leaving their hands free for greater comfort or the enterprising dispersal of flyers. But can you imagine just how much human flotsam you're going to have to put up with when you spend all day standing stock still in the middle of the world's busiest shopping thoroughfare? You're fair game for every tramp, lost tourist, idiotic practical joker and random nutter who shares the street with you. The thin-skinned and gullible do not last long. There's also the boredom to consider. What little novelty value being a human signpost has must evaporate after about two minutes, so what the hell do you do with yourself after that? Even the most avid people-watcher in the world must be howling for solitude after half an hour. On the bright side you're working outdoors, you get to meet a lot of people and you never have to go to meetings or come up with ideas to impress the boss. You never have to worry about promotion or pretend you like your colleagues, because you don't have any. And how many people who work in advertising can say that?

UNOFFICIAL JOB TITLE >> Fruitloop
WAGES >> £10.00 an hour, all the juice you can drink
HOURS >> 8 a.m. – 4 p.m. weekdays, with two breaks
UNIFORM >> Large yellow banana outfit and a pair of yellow tights
SPECIALIST SKILLS >> A permanent smile, love of repetition and
a well-developed sense of the absurd

The juice-bar business is booming in London. No longer satisfied with tea and diet Coke, the thirsty and well-heeled workers of the City are now demanding a huge range of thirst-quenching nectars, preferably healthy, freshly squeezed and made from exotic and expensive fruits. So is born the juice bar, where everything from bananas to wheatgrass is peeled, chopped, blended to within an inch of its life, then served up in plastic beakers for several quid a go.

Competition is fierce – it's a lucrative market and it's easy to get into. Anyone can crush a strawberry. So in order to stand out from the crowd, the marketing wizards at one particular chain have gone for one of the oldest tricks in the book – the funny costume. Every year they hire a few desperate folk to dress up as fruit, stand on the street and hand out promotional flyers.

The banana costume is made of cheap artificial yellow fur, like a fairground teddy bear, with two leg holes towards the bottom of the banana's curve and a hole for the head at the top. This is where the sections of imitation peel sit on the wearer's shoulders. Before this can be donned, however, the headgear, or peeled section of the banana must be worn. It fits over the head with a hole for the face, and there are two armholes below, which secure it in place. Then, after the yellow tights have been put on, the bulk of the banana can be slipped into place.

Movement is severely restricted in the costume, as is the wearer's field of vision. The wearer cannot turn his head to see, but must rotate his entire body. The curve of the banana also protrudes from between the legs in an alarmingly phallic manner. Thus adorned, the humble banana man must stand outside tube stations in the City of London, proffering leaflets to City boys and the phrase 'Free smoothie?' to all who pass. Some are polite – they smile, take the leaflet and pass on. Others look horrified, as if they are about to be press-ganged into some amusing fruit-related street pantomime, and take comically evasive measures to avoid eye contact. Then there are the tourists from countries where zany behaviour is at a premium and who delight in having their photograph taken with a big London banana.

Some, however, are not so nice. The schoolchildren who, taking cruel advantage of the banana's limited vision, attempt to light the tail of the costume from behind, provoking streams of language unbefitting a cheery ambassador of fruit-related drinks. There is of course the scourge of many a London worker on the move – white van man, whose Doppler-effect insults trail loudly from the passing traffic with a well-timed 'wwwaaaaaaannnkkaa'. But those who take pity are the worst; the psychotherapeutic do-gooders armed with emotional sticking plasters. 'Ooh, love, what happened to you?' they say, or 'I hope they're paying you enough for this, mate.' They put hands on shoulders, they offer commiseration and, nine times out of ten, they don't even take a leaflet. So next time you see someone dressed as a banana, or a big Swiss cheese, or a cuddly comedy bear, don't pity them, don't try to help them – just take one of their leaflets and get on with your life. That's all they really want.

UNOFFICIAL JOB TITLE >> Toilet Monitor
WAGES >> Whatever you can get
HOURS >> 6 p.m. until whenever the place closes
UNIFORM >> Shirt, trousers and a creepy smile
SPECIALIST SKILLS >> Perfume handling, towel passing, lollipop management and grinning inanely for hours on end. An underdeveloped sense of smell may also be useful.

I quit!

As clubbing, dancing and general merriment have become more and more mainstream after the dark days of rave, clubs have become ever more sophisticated in their attempts to outdo the competition. And so was born the toilet attendant, long a feature of many a continental convenience but a relative newcomer to these shores. It used to be the case that you would only find an actual employee in the toilets somewhere really swanky, like the nice old boy who works the gents at the Savoy, but clubs and bars soon cottoned on to the idea that you could make the place look really classy if you bought a couple of bottles of CK One and a tub of lollies, then hired some poor stiff to hand people their towels at the sink.

It's caught on big time, and now you see them everywhere, even in ghastly chain pubs with cheap beer and bad carpets. Trouble is, the clientele aren't always that appreciative of the service. So the poor attendant's job is to stand around in the loos of a huge, cheap boozer on a Friday night and watch people piss, fart, dribble onto their shoes, belch, fall over, throw up and everything else that attends a night of cheap and heavy drinking. And that's just the Ladies. Imagine what it's like in the Gents. If the punters bother to wash their hands at all, the chances are they're not about to bung anyone a quid for the luxury of not having to pull their own paper out of the machine or to spray them with cheap cologne. As the evening wears on, the crowd gets

drunker, louder, stupider and increasingly inaccurate at the urinals, not to mention potentially aggressive when encouraged to part with money for the privilege of taking a wizz.

While many people assume that the attendant is a paid member of staff, in many cases they have to pay the venue for the right to get the bathroom concession and have to supply all their own toiletries as well, meaning that the little silver dish optimistically sprinkled with pound coins is probably the only money they're making. So spare a thought next time you pop in to spend a penny – at least you're pissing voluntarily, instead of having it taken out of you.

My Story: I Was a Glastonbury Steward by journalist and writer Peter Paphides

One of the perks of joining the Labour Party when I was an undergraduate was that, if you so desired, you could volunteer to be a steward at Glastonbury. In the spring of 1992, with my finals looming, this was enough to politicise me. We'd never been to the mother of all festivals, my pals and I, and this seemed like a good way to wave goodbye to our cosseted subsidised life and combine work with assiduous patronage of the spicy cider stall. When we got there, our duties were explained to us. We had to do three eight-hour shifts at a variety of gates. We were to check people's wrists and make sure their wristbands were securely fastened. One of these shifts had to be a night shift. Now, I know that, in the general scheme of things, this doesn't amount to much work. This was 1992, after all – one of the hottest Glastos on record. But in 1992, 'Madchester' had spawned an unpleasant new generation of bacon-faced scallies whose sole aim in life was to sell Oxo cubes to naive students and convince stewards that their wristbands had 'fallen off'. I dimly remembered these people; they were the types I had attempted to avoid by staying in higher education. That said, in the daytime, people who failed the audition to play maracas for The Farm were no more than an irritant.

The night shift was a different story. Just uneventful enough to make you really appreciate how improbably chilly the Vale of Avalon can get even in the middle of summer, but once in a while an ogre in Stussy would amble up to the perimeter and tell me that they too had lost their wristband. Of course, it wasn't my job to turn them away. Well, actually it was, but the security steward behind me would always intervene if Stussy Guy got shirty. Quite how those same security stewards managed to be on a toilet break every time I needed them was something I never got around to asking.

Maybe I was too depressed. Three shifts was nothing. But it was enough to turn me into the biggest curmudgeon on the festival site (Morrissey had pulled out at the last minute). In the end, I finished my final shift, brushed the spiders off my belongings and hitched home. As I left, I could hear the unbearably ironic sound of The Levellers getting 20,000 festival-goers to sing, 'There's only one way of life/And that's your own.' Realising that my innate cynicism could be put to much better use, I became a music journalist. Ensuing Glastonbury festivals have been rather more enjoyable as a result.

I Quit!

UNOFFICIAL JOB TITLE >> The Happy Clamper
WAGES >> £5.00 per hour
HOURS >> 6 a.m. – 6 p.m. in rotating shifts
UNIFORM >> Large fluorescent jacket and trousers
SPECIALIST SKILLS >> Accurate timekeeping and a heart of utter granite

No one likes to go to hospital. Patients, staff, they'd all rather be somewhere else entirely. There's nothing pleasant about the experience for anyone. Every day the relatives dutifully pull up at the hospital to visit the sick and the dying, bearing the spare pyjamas, the magazines and Lucozade that cement the transactions between the sick and the well. It's frequently harrowing. So imagine how much better everyone feels when they come back out again to find that, because they're ten minutes over the time on their parking ticket, someone's attaching a clamp to their front wheel and won't take it off for less than £60? Welcome to the world of the hospital parking attendant, gatekeeper at the doors of public misery.

'I'm not a cruel person in the least,' says Brian. 'I've always wanted to be a musician, a guitarist, but I hit a financial ebb a few years back and took the parking job.' As you can probably imagine, things weren't quite as easy for Brian as he first imagined. 'I'd pictured myself sitting in a little booth, smiling and handing out tickets to people.' The reality was somewhat different. Keen to use their car parks as a way of generating much-needed revenue, the hospital in question insisted that a zero-tolerance policy should be levied against those who overstayed their welcome. As such, Brian found himself issued with a shopping trolley full of wheel clamps, a ticket book and some stickers and was dispatched around the car park to hunt the offenders down like scurvy dogs. As with most car-related enforcement, people tended to react rather badly when confronted. 'On my very first day, I was threatened with extreme violence twice, then later someone actually swung at my head with a tyre wrench.' So far, so normal – after all, people get very upset when you mess with their cars. But the deal breaker for Brian was that his particular patch of the car park was that which served the hospital's Intensive Care Unit. The desperate nature of most people's attendance was such that many simply forgot about their cars altogether. When they eventually came stumbling out in a haze of grief, they would then be confronted with a big green clamp on their cars and a hefty fine to boot.

'There must have been three or four people in that week who were so "dented" when they came to pay for clamp removal that it was obvious they'd only just been bereaved,' continues a thoroughly repentant Brian, shuddering at the memory. 'The guilt from having to put them through a merciless process of form filling, fine taking and then making them wait until the supervisor came back with the clamp keys made me feel really, really low.' A tempting combination of ultra-violence and massive, overbearing guilt in daily doses – that's life as a hospital car-park wheel-clamper.

UNOFFICIAL JOB TITLE >> Aroma Roamer
WAGES >> Minimum
HOURS >> 10 a.m. – 6 p.m. plus extensive commuting time
UNIFORM >> Cheap shiny suit for the boys, something smart with a bit of cleavage for the girls
SPECIALIST SKILLS >> Strong legs, a quality fake smile and endless reserves of love for the product

You can't always see the hotspots, but they're there if you know how to look for them. Those places where crowds of moving people – shoppers, travellers, tourists – take a small breather from being frenetically propelled from one place to another by signs and cleverly designed walkways to take stock of where they are. Places with benches are good, as are food courts, underneath big information boards, that sort of thing. When shoppers stop to stare, confused by fluorescent lights and overloaded with data, that's the best time to strike.

'Nina Ricci, madam?' asks the young man in the cheap suit, advancing with a grim smile and determined posture towards his intended victim. Armed with only a sample bottle and hope, he attempts to complete the holy trinity of the perfume sampler. First comes the initial spray of the perfume onto the punter, intended to elicit a delighted response. Second stage should complete the sale of a small bottle. Thirdly – and this is the ultimate prize – he wants a completed customer card bulging with highly prized demographic information. That's when the bonus money really starts rolling in.

Those days, however, are rare. People are mostly suspicious of being approached by a stranger, especially in the Southeast, and supplying him with information that tells everything from what magazines you regularly

purchase to your education history. He's been punched several times by irate boyfriends who've emerged from a shop or a toilet to find their partners being flirted with by some 'perfumed chancer' or, on the days when they're doing an aftershave promotion, by blokes who think he's gay. Women respond very well at first, but have been known to start shrieking because he won't give them a phone number or come back to their houses for afternoon entertainment. He's learning to weed out the real customers from the time-wasters, but it didn't come easily. Hours were spent watching his commission run down the drain while he talked enthusiastically to the lonely and the mad, the poor and friendless – people who just wanted to chat.

It's the hours that really bite, though. Whenever other people have free time, that's when he's out and about. Lunchtimes, Saturday mornings, big outdoor events, Christmas sales. Up and down the country, zig-zagging from Bluewater to Thurrock, Heathrow to Oxford St, he eats from motorway service stations and Travelodges, mostly sleeping in the back of the car to and from work. He reckons he's been around the M25 over three hundred times. Most people don't last that long, but those who do might be in line for a supervisor's job in a year or two – a real office, team of their own, only popping out to sites once a week, maybe even a chance to get into marketing. Depends on how next month's stint at Luton Arndale Centre goes. Deep breath, smile on, purposeful stride – 'Nina Ricci, madam?'

My Story: I Was a Record Shop Salesman by Andrew Mueller – writer and broadcaster

Working in a small suburban record shop, as I did for a couple of years in my late teens at home in Sydney, is not, it must be conceded, the toughest row to hoe. There's no heavy lifting; the hours are agreeable and, if the owner isn't in, you can listen to whatever you like. In fact, only one thing prevents working in a record shop from being a thoroughly pleasant way to earn a buck, but that one thing is so utterly, soul-crushingly, will-to-live-sappingly dreadful that there were many days when I contemplated the lot of coal-miners, ditch-diggers and urinal cake salesmen with a certain wistful envy. I refer, of course, to the general public.

Whenever someone proclaims their all-embracing love of people, you can be reasonably sure that they're insane, and completely certain that they have never worked in a record shop. No other occupation exposes you so often, so unrelentingly, to the fathomless abyss of human stupidity. People would come in and hum something they'd heard on the radio. They were always completely tone deaf, and, after enduring 30 seconds of their monotonous drone, we'd send them away with a copy of Nick Cave's 'The Mercy Seat'; not one of them ever complained. Others would approach the counter with a description of a record so vague that it would scarcely have been less use to us if they'd pronounced it in Navajo. 'I don't know what it's called,' one idiot told us, 'or who it's by, but I know it has a green cover.' After considerable further interrogation – it was a slow afternoon – we deduced that what he wanted was The Smiths' The Queen Is Dead. And, if he didn't want it, that's what he got.

There were certain subtle revenges available to us. Under the counter behind the cash register was a doorbell switch, marked with the words 'Customer Eject Button'; while it was not, sadly, actually connected to any apparatus capable of launching Tracy Chapman fans through the skylight, pressing it was a surprisingly effective psychological release. Or there was always plain rudeness. Many was the time that some cheerful, middle-aged-before-his-time-middle-manager would swagger in, his tie raffishly loosened, and ask we trendily dishevelled adolescents behind the counter what the new Sting album was like. And many was the time we wound them up as painfully as only the truth can. 'Bloody awful,' we'd reply, affecting an archly disdainful expression that clearly communicated that anyone even thinking of buying the new Sting album might just as well buy a pair of shoes with zippers and spend their days mumbling about the war in post-office queues. Lest anyone think that all of the above is only what's to be expected from consumers of rock music, the single most moronic enquiry I ever fielded was from someone browsing the classical section.

'I see you have *The Four Seasons* by Vivaldi,' she said.
'Yes,' I replied, fighting the urge to ask her if she could tell me why every person who ever bought it was, like her good self, a woman with riotous hair who reeked of patchouli.
'Do you,' she continued, 'have it by anyone else?'

To this day, I regret very little as much as I regret not having the presence of mind to tell her no, but that I could heartily recommend Beethoven's Fifth by Tchaikovsky, or Bach's Toccata and Fugue in D Minor by Mahler. Instead, I stifled an involuntary shriek, and made haste for the stockroom, leaving the poor bewildered woman alone with Iggy Pop's 'Instinct' on the shop stereo, almost, but not quite eclipsing the incredulous laughter of myself and my colleagues.

CHAPTER TWO

THE FACTORY FLOOR

THE MAN WHO BUILDS A FACTORY BUILDS A TEMPLE, THAT THE MAN WHO WORKS THERE WORSHIPS THERE, AND TO EACH IS DUE, NOT SCORN AND BLAME, BUT REVERENCE AND PRAISE. **CALVIN COOLIDGE**

I quit!

Yeah, right. One can bet fairly safely that the author of that little gem never found himself on the business end of a broom in a woodworking factory. Or shovelling additives and whey powder into a vat of mechanically recovered meat destined for cheap pies and sausages. Everyone knows that working in a factory is, for the most part, noisy work that strains the muscles, numbs the brain and pays barely enough for a much-needed snifter at the end of the long working week. As the globalisation of the economy continues its relentless pace, we in the UK have seen more and more of our factory jobs exported to those who need the money even more than we do, but in this chapter we take a look at some of the places where it's still possible to get down and dirty on the production line. No doubt many parts of the country feature brightly lit factories with long breaks, nice music and a canteen full of comfy chairs and televisions, but we're not really interested in them. This is about the business end of business – the dirty, gritty and downright ridiculous things people are required to do to aid the manufacture, of, well, stuff. Roll up your sleeves and get stuck in.

UNOFFICIAL JOB TITLE » Soap Slave
WAGES » Minimum wage, no overtime but more money on night shifts
HOURS » 8 a.m – 4p.m. Monday to Friday
UNIFORM » Blue industrial denim trousers, company polo shirt.
No long hair or jewellery
SPECIALIST SKILLS » Heat-resistant hands, a tolerance for laundry
soap, no hang-ups about other people's stains

I Quit!

All over the country, in every city, town and village, someone needs the industrial laundrette. From the iffy-bowelled residents of care homes to the untidy guests at airport hotels, the industrial laundrette serves them all, collecting their dirty towels, linen, bathmats, dishcloths, chefs' whites and uniforms in big blue sacks and depositing them back the next day, cleaned, folded and shrink-wrapped in plastic.

The laundry is housed in a big warehouse space built of breezeblock and corrugated iron at the edge of an industrial estate. Housed within its walls is a huge production line, beginning at one end where the lorries drop off the dirty stuff and ending at the other, where the clean items are dispatched. There is row upon row of giant cylindrical washers with drums big enough for a man to climb into, and dryers to match. Huge lines of hooks zigzag across the ceiling, carrying bulging bags of laundry from one section to another. Wet towels are moved by the half-ton in giant blue baskets on wheels from the spin dryer to the folding machine, which looks like the inside of a giant piano, their banks of sloping wires carrying the towels upwards.

You don't know boredom until you've worked on the folding machine. Eight hours a day of reaching into a basket, taking a towel, laying it flat on the wires and THAT'S IT. You don't even fold the things – that's the machine's job. Stacking them, wrapping them in their plastic bundles – all someone else's

job. You just put them on the belt. Even worse than that, they're all exactly the same shape and colour. To save money, all the laundry's customers buy their generic towels from the same place for the cheapest price. No variety at all – no floral patterns or gaudy superhero prints, just white with a red stripe at the top. All day long, forever.

It's hot too – really hot. The combination of hot water and constant spin-drying fills the place with a persistent damp fug. It smells of soap, of sweat and of dirt. At the business end, where they open the bags of dirty stuff, it smells of much worse. In the summer, when the sun beats down onto the thin steel roof, it sometimes gets so hot they have to make everyone come in two hours early, to stop the older staff from fainting.

Quality Control Operative

Richard Wild (author's brother)

UNOFFICIAL JOB TITLE >> Mr Crispy
WAGES >> Minimum
HOURS >> 8 a.m. – 6 p.m. Monday to Friday
UNIFORM >> Paper boiler suit, paper shoe covers and a hairnet
**SPECIALIST SKILLS >> A huge appetite for fried snacks and
a tolerance for acne**

I once made crisps, in a factory, of course. Upon arrival at a medium-sized industrial unit, the line manager took me into a changing room where I had to don a paper boiler suit, paper overshoes and a hairnet (despite pointing out the fact that having a skinhead minimised the possibility of follicular fallout into their product, and that the net made me and everyone else look like we were on our way to enjoy 'medication time'). After this, I shuffled behind the manager to the factory floor, which consisted of:

1. A potato-peeling machine
2. A potato-slicing machine
3. The largest vat of hot oil I have ever seen (about 6' x 4' and 3.5' deep)
4. An equally large draining tray for cooked crisps
5. Some cement mixers
6. A 10' x 4' metal tray on a bench – my section

Basically, the sliced spuds were dumped en masse into the deep-fat fryer, which bubbled menacingly and produced miniature geysers and considerable amounts of oily steam. An old man then stirred them continuously. He had clearly been doing the job for a while because he was (a) bright pink, (b) exceptionally shiny-skinned and seemingly devoid of arm and facial hair, and (c) afflicted with some kind of horrific latent acne. Whether or not he received any extra remuneration for enduring this Dante-esque nightmare, I'll never know, because it was too hot to get within six feet of him. I'll bet he didn't like sunbathing, though. After being fried the crisps were drained and then, rather oddly, chucked into the row of cement mixers next to me. I was disappointed to find out that this was the flavouring section: once full, the mixers were cranked up and an employee would pour in 'salt and vinegar' or 'chicken' or 'hedgehog' (seriously) flavoured powder, which came in large plastic paint tubs. A key element of this person's position was controlling the strength of the flavouring, which was achieved through eating a great deal of lukewarm crisps. Given that the guy manning the mixers when I was there was stick-thin (but spotty, like everyone else), I can only assume the previous taster had recently died from cholesterol-induced heart failure.

So on to my allotted section: quality control. Skinny, spotty, tasting man would periodically tip out the contents of the mixers on to the large metal tray in front of me, at which point I had to look through them for defective produce. When I say 'them', I mean a cumulative mountain of sticky, powder-covered fried potato about two feet high that filled the tray to the corners. The manager informed me that each tray load was made up of approximately one million individual crisps, and that I had to look for defectives of one of three scientific categories: (1) Stickers: when two or more fried slices had stuck together; (2) Eyers: crisps with any black bits in them; and (3) Sticky Eyers: take a wild leap of the imagination. In an eight-hour day, to check a million crisps equates to sifting through just over 2,000 crisps a minute, or more precisely, 34.72 crisps per second – about the contents of an average bag. It was totally hellish. Upon seeing my jaw bounce off the shop floor, the manager said, as if it was the true incentive of the job, that I was free to eat as many as I liked.

After that day, I didn't eat a single crisp for weeks, as just the sight of one packet would conjure up the image of the alopecial geriatric lobster, with buboes sizzling gently on his rosy cheeks and forehead.

Pallet Wrapper

UNOFFICIAL JOB TITLE >> Crate Boy
WAGES >> £6.00 per hour
HOURS >> 6 p.m. – 6a.m. Monday to Thursday
UNIFORM >> Not required – earplugs mandatory
SPECIALIST SKILLS >> Sight and one working finger

We can confidently make the claim that most people don't devote much time to thinking about where cardboard comes from. It's such a common, everyday commodity, like plastic bags or glass bottles, that we take its existence for granted. But it has to be made, and lurking on industrial estates up and down the country is the exciting prospect that is the cardboard factory.

Before you get too excited, this job doesn't involve actually making boxes or life-size cardboard celebrities for bookshop windows, or any of the other wonderful things that cardboard can be used for. No folding or printing here, just the cardboard itself, in huge, long flat strips. The smell of the place we researched is actually quite pleasant, and a lot of people remark that the aroma reminds them of a take-away pizza. It's actually more that take-away pizzas smell like the factory, because that sweet, moist waft you get when you open a pizza box is mainly the smell of the wet, hot cardboard the box is made of rather than the pizza itself.

At one end of the long factory are the reams of paper from which the cardboard is fashioned – huge cylinders of paper that weigh several tons and have to be carried onto the production line by forklifts. The older workers tell horror stories of the 'old days' – of falling reams and broken limbs. The reams are loaded onto axles and drawn into the presses, which moisten and fold and press and dry until huge sheets of card come out the other end to be sliced up into portions . . .

. . . which is where the pallet wrapper comes in. Customers order their piles of cardboard sheets in different sizes, each appropriate for a different kind of box. Each size of pile has a corresponding pallet on which it must rest to fit into the back of the delivery lorry. Our man stands at the front of a conveyor belt surrounded by piles of different pallets. As a pile of card approaches, the right pallet is selected and placed at the end of the line. The card plops onto it, and then the wrapper must press a button, activating the machine that binds the card to the pallet with plastic straps.

The monotony is overwhelming. Because of the noise of the machines it's impossible to have a radio on and, besides, all workers have to wear earplugs anyway. The nearest human being is at least ten feet away. It's very hot and steamy and the sickly-sweet smell of cheap glue permeates the atmosphere. Even taking a break for a quick smoke is a chore, as the cardboard factory is obviously a fairly major fire risk, so smokers must troop 200 yards across the delivery bay to a tiny metal shack full of sand buckets.

The production line cannot stop moving, as it takes several minutes to restart and costs a great deal of money, so mistakes are severely frowned upon. Sometimes the neat piles of card slip over and scatter, forcing everyone to leap from their posts and rush to the pile, frantically putting it all back into place and swearing at the tops of their voices. Other times the wrapper misjudges the pallet size and the binding straps cut deeply into the pile, ruining the card. That's rare though. Mostly it's just card, mile after mile of it, for twelve hours a night with no conversation.

UNOFFICIAL JOB TITLE >> Acid Head
WAGES >> £3.00 per hour
HOURS >> 9 a.m. – 6 p.m. Monday to Friday
UNIFORM >> Not supplied
SPECIALIST SKILLS >> A steady hand and an ability to spiritually transcend one's immediate environment

Aciiid! The cry of many a raver in the late 1980s has different connotations for Mike, who spent some time in an industrial battery-acid factory during his student years. Shoved in a freezing cold, bleak warehouse in a faceless, grey industrial park somewhere on the outskirts of London, he was tasked by the surly line manager with filling large batteries with the kind of solution serial killers use to dispose of their evidence. Needless to say there was no training or protective gear provided and, when he complained, the multi-chinned manager summarily ignored him, continuing to march at a furious pace down the aisles of acrid aluminium and burning plastic. It was only when he threatened to take it up with the union that he stopped and whirled round, shoving himself fully into what Californians call one's 'personal space'. He set about bellowing halitosis-coated expletives at the poor student – worse than the ammonia stench of the solution that, for the subsequent weeks, would become horribly familiar. On the second day, Mike knew he was in for an unpleasant time when his trainers started to smoke. By the end of the week, his clothes were full of holes, his trainers ruined and his face had taken on a deeply unpleasant blotchy appearance.

UNOFFICIAL JOB TITLE >> Hinge and Bracket Racket
WAGES >> £5.00 per hour, with a £10 'bonus' if you show up
on time five days in a row
HOURS >> 8 a.m. – 5 p.m. Monday to Friday
UNIFORM >> Company polo shirt
SPECIALIST SKILLS >> Nimble and burn-resistant fingers,
a total and complete lack of ambition

I Quit!

Britain's fading seaside towns have a certain sleazy charm. Battered by inclement weather and the very good chance that they will never reclaim the glory days of centuries past, they sit, decaying beautifully, waiting for regeneration. Behind the guest houses and bingo halls of one particular seafront, however, lurks an industrial estate wherein nestles a big shack fashioned from breeze blocks and corrugated, well, something – not iron – it looks more like papier-mâché.

Every morning at about 7.50 a.m., the workers start shuffling towards the entrance. Some of them are to be found lounging on pallets out front, grabbing a few last gasps of a roll-up before the shift starts or, in some cases, taking a shifty restorative nip of something wrapped in brown paper. Once inside they take to their various stations and begin assembling the boxes of hinges, screws and other myriad parts necessary for the construction of what they produce: door and window handles for the double-glazing industry.

As with all manual-labour environments, the radio plays all day every day. Beneath the industrial din one might hear snatches of recognisable songs, so you may find yourself singing along when noise levels permit such revelry. The handful of students and others of a slightly alternative bent who have passed through the doors have always campaigned for Radio 1 and have always been defeated. The local station, with its cuddly animal logo, rigorous adherence to the 'amusing noises' model of the breakfast show, and ad breaks for – that's right – double glazing, every ten minutes, continues to dominate and seems to play the same ten songs all day long.

Management have worked out, as the fast-food chains did years ago, that the more skill is required of the worker, the more expensive the manufacturing process becomes. Break the thing down into as many separate jobs as possible, pay each person a minimum to do the same thing over and over, day in day out, and the product remains consistent. With the added bonus that no one need be extensively trained or even permanently employed. So one guy puts the screws in the hinges, another puts the cogs inside the handle mechanisms – each person doing one tiny part before passing it on for its next step towards becoming a completed handle. For those really up against it, there's a home-working scheme. Take a box of a thousand parts home and spend all your free time putting them together in front of the telly for an extra £50 a week.

Needless to say, the boredom factor is somewhat on the high side, and not all employees are 100 per cent career-minded, either. The old soak on hinges pops off to the toilet every ten minutes for a swig of something or other, and is best not approached after midday. The all-pervading atmosphere is one of shiftiness. Various other low-level hustlers on the production line spend their 30-minute lunch breaks on mobile phones, fishing bags out of their cars or popping off on dubious errands. One source told me there's a lot of speed being taken too – it makes the day go that bit quicker.

At five o' clock, they all shuffle out – hands sore, clothes covered in metal filings and dust – to sink gratefully into a chair and a bottle of beer, or directly to the pub. All so some oily rep with a bad suit can ring you up at an inconvenient time to ask you if you want your house double-glazed, or whether that lovely garden could do with a conservatory.

Product Stress Tester

UNOFFICIAL JOB TITLE >> Handjobber
WAGES >> £6.50 per hour
HOURS >> 8 a.m. – 6 p.m. Monday to Friday
UNIFORM >> Hairnet and overalls to maintain the sterile atmosphere
SPECIALIST SKILLS >> Nothing too demanding. Just keep thinking about the love

Once upon a time, contraception was a decidedly risky enterprise, not to mention something of an uncomfortable one. From the restrictive and impractical miseries of the chastity belt to the considerably off-putting notion of using a sheep's bladder as a prophylactic, you can't blame anyone who decided to just risk it instead. Even as far back as a century ago, the height of contraceptive technology was a covering for the male member made of leather, which seems not only potentially uncomfortable for the recipient but so lacking in sensation for the deliverer as to be pointless. Of course, there's always the rhythm method, but that particular rhythm seems to have been more efficient for conception rather than contraception.

So the condom must have been a blessing. The advent of rubber technologies may have transformed the industrial world as we know it with everything from tyres to waterproof shoes, but surely the jimmy hat is the very height of its achievements. Now you might imagine that all kinds of complicated computerised equipment is utilised in the manufacturing process of condoms – CAD, stress testing, that kind of thing. It probably is. But, for one unfortunate employee, there's no escaping the business end of the sex business. As any fellow who has donned a condom will attest, there's not only the hurdle of getting the damn thing on . . . as enthusiasm increases, the condom can also display a worrying tendency to work itself loose, a fact often discovered when it's too late to do anything about it.

So, to counter this problem, the factory in which our condom tester works is equipped with a special device. Mounted on a large pneumatic arm is a mould designed to match the average male member in every anatomical detail. Facing this, as you may have guessed, is a lovingly crafted and startlingly life like latex vagina. Following successful trials with (honestly) a broad sample of German prostitutes, a new design has been put forward which attempts to address the problem of slippage.

From morning till night, this particularly lovely job involves applying a thick layer of grease to both the imitation penis and its intended destination, firing up the machine, and then watching it hammer in and out while taking careful note of how many thrusts are successfully completed before the condom begins to slip. Whether or not the machine's accurate depiction of the act of love includes giving up halfway through and quietly blaming the three pints earlier that evening, or simply slowing down for a bit to get its breath back is something our researchers were unable to ascertain.

Quite what it must do for anyone's sex life to spend all day greasing up a fake set of genitals and then watching them slam into each other for eight hours a day is anyone's guess, although it can't lend itself to any great deal of sensitivity in the bedroom. That's if the poor sods can even be bothered to indulge with the scarring images of mechanically assisted sex burned into their brains.

Product Stress Tester

Fish Factory Cleaner

UNOFFICIAL JOB TITLE >> Absolutely Gutted
WAGES >> £5.50 per hour
HOURS >> 6 p.m. – 6 a.m. Monday to Thursday
UNIFORM >> Full body suit, face mask and shoe covers
SPECIALIST SKILLS >> Iron stomach

I quit!

Fancy cookery is all the rage these days. Media watchers can barely escape being assaulted from all sides by beautifully arranged and photographed information and advice about how to buy, prepare and cook food. Celebrity chefs gurn from our TV screens; good domestic cooks are elevated to the status of minor deities, and the visiting alien might be forgiven for believing that the average British family regularly sits down of an evening to tuck into a freshly made three-course meal, consisting only of the freshest organic ingredients, lovingly prepared to an ancient Tuscan recipe by delicate and skilled hands.

Do they bollocks. In the main, the British public's seemingly insatiable appetite for reading about and watching good food being prepared has yet to translate to the dinner table. Get down to the local supermarket and watch – it's all trolleys loaded with biscuits, crisps, chemical-laden cooking sauces and tinned and packaged convenience goods. Instead of a smiling, hearty fishmonger holding the latest fresh catch by the tail and suggesting perhaps a dill sauce with that, madam, there's a surly teenager lumping polystyrene packs of tired salmon into the chill cabinet. We've still got a long way to go . . . which suits the bosses of the UK's fish factories down to the ground. Its workers are at the front line of the fish business. Not for them the firm flesh of a fresh cod to be delicately skinned and fried for a delicious supper. They

handle the industrial fish, the scrag-end of the day's catch, to be scaled, gutted, beheaded, cut into fillets, shaped and then frozen solid and squashed into boxes with those chemically laden sauces, better to facilitate its transport to all the far-flung corners of the UK.

Hundreds of thousands of fish come through the doors every day and, as one would expect, it's a messy business. They have to be converted from whole fish into convenient frozen chunks as quickly as possible, which puts pressure on all the factory workers. No one really likes the job, but our particular concern is with the cleaner. As the fish make their way through the production line they are washed, then their skin and heads are removed. These are funnelled off the line to be packed and shipped to various buyers such as the cat-food and cosmetics industry. Then the inedible guts must be removed before the fish is washed again and cut. As no one wants the guts; these are removed and placed on a big drip tray, which in turn drops them into a huge central vat beneath the line, located in a stainless steel cube with a giant plug at the bottom. Our unfortunate employee's job is, at the end of the working day, to suit up so that no fish matter can get into his eyes, ears or anywhere else. He is then lowered into the steel gut room with a high-pressure hose. He cannot leave until it's sparkling clean. The first and most obviously horrible thing is the smell – a concentrated, intense aroma of rotting maritime matter – flesh, excrement and seawater, without the benefit of refrigeration. Secondly, the hours that pass between the dropping of the guts and the cleaning of them means that a great deal of the fish matter dries and sticks to the walls and floor, requiring no little scraping from the cleaner. Thirdly, when the room is eventually clean, there are four more to be tackled before the shift is over.

Light relief is provided only by one's fellow workers' jocular banter, so you'd better pray that you are sharing your shift with some Perrier Award-winning talent. There's also the much-talked-about trick they've learned from the local trawlermen regarding the use of a skate wing. It has a gill that very closely resembles the more intimate parts of a woman's anatomy . . . we'll leave the rest to your imagination. How the nights must fly by.

Timber Yard Cleaner

UNOFFICIAL JOB TITLE >> Eternal Sweeper
WAGES >> £3.00 per hour
HOURS >> 8 a.m. – 2 p.m. Monday to Friday
UNIFORM >> Trousers clipped at the ankles, rubber gloves and a dust mask
SPECIALIST SKILLS >> Iron lungs, strong forearms and a hefty grasp of irony

In a small village nestling in a picturesque part of the English countryside, there lies a modest industrial unit set back from the road, and conveniently located about 200 yards from the pub. Housed within this unit is the local timber yard, full of lathes, saws, tools and, obviously, timber. As a teenager in this village, employment opportunities were few and far between. I'd already been unceremoniously sacked from my job as a dishwasher at the nearby hotel and restaurant in what I perceived to be extremely unfair circumstances. Having taken the weekend off without telling anyone to go and get wasted with my mates, I returned to find the boss no longer required my surly services. The cheek of it! Smarting with teenage outrage, I soon realised that my weekly dope and cider bills were not going to be met by my meagre allowance and that other employment would have to be found.

So, when I saw the sign saying 'Cleaner required – 30 hours a week' on the window of the timber yard, I thought it might suit very nicely. A bit early in the morning but it did leave plenty of time the rest of the day for loafing, drinking and other seamy pursuits. The wages, at three pounds an hour, weren't exactly what I hoped for, but I wasn't really in a position to argue. I popped in to have a word with the boss, a genial tubby old boy called Jim, who gave me the once over and decreed me fit for the job. 'We were expecting a woman, actually,' he said, eyeing my long hair with a mixture of disdain and amusement, 'but I suppose you'll do. See you tomorrow.'

I should have known things wouldn't work out when I showed up on the first day. The staff were sitting around in the filthy portacabin that passed for a break room, propped up on bricks next to the main yard. As I stepped inside, half-a-dozen swarthy-necked timber workers stopped laughing at whatever bovine joke they'd been enjoying seconds previously and stared at me. 'This is our new cleaner,' said Jim, the strain evident in his cheerful tone as the collective disappointment resounded around the room that the lecherous thrill of having a female vigorously sweeping the floor within grabbing distance had been denied them. A few half-hearted grunts were thrown in my direction and I was never directly spoken to again.

The job, such as it was, consisted of cleaning up around the timber yard. Now bear in mind that all day, every day, this yard basically slices wood from big bits into smaller bits, occasionally stopping to glue some of them to each other. There is no such thing as a clean timber yard. It doesn't matter how much you sweep it, dust it, wipe it, whatever, ten minutes later it looks exactly the same as it did when you started. The sawdust gets up your nose, down your throat, into your underwear and your socks. Every time you blow your nose, a horrendous mixture of snot and sawdust fills your handkerchief, or, if you're a timber cutter, your shirt sleeve. And splinters . . . don't talk to me about splinters. The company policy stated that employees were supposed to wear dust masks while working, but I believed (quite rightly) that everyone thought I was a massive middle-class Jessie, so if they didn't wear them I was damned if I was going to. Unfortunately, this didn't work too well for an asthmatic and I spent every morning after waking coughing like a tramp for a good ten minutes. After a couple of weeks of this torture, good sense prevailed and I threw in the towel – to the collective relief of all. I've never been back to industrial work again, and it doesn't miss me one bit.

Adam Cousins

CHAPTER THREE

FIELDS OF DREAMS

WITH THE INTRODUCTION OF AGRICULTURE MANKIND ENTERED UPON A LONG PERIOD OF MEANNESS, MISERY, AND MADNESS, FROM WHICH THEY ARE ONLY NOW BEING FREED BY THE BENEFICENT OPERATION OF THE MACHINE.

BERTRAND RUSSELL

Anyone browsing the supermarket shelves these days would be forgiven for thinking that there's no such thing as agriculture any more – that we get all our foods from large industrial outlets that cook up vats of synthetic cheese gloop, bake plastic bread and make those neat little toys that go inside Kinder eggs. The time when families would grow most of their own vegetables and keep a few chickens or pigs about the place are long gone, replaced by 24-hour supermarkets and fast-food joints. But all those burger buns and pre-cut, shrink-wrapped carrots have to come from somewhere.

So in this chapter we take a look at those who toil in the fields, picking and plucking the goods that end up, after drying or packing or being ferried hundreds of miles, in our fridges and cupboards. Not for us the romanticism of the wind gently rolling through golden fields of wheat, or the heartily laden table of country fayre to feed the shiny workers at the end of the honest day. We're looking at the bottom of the rung in agribusiness, the kinds of jobs that no machine can replace, no matter how much the bosses would like them to. So get up nice and early, put on some stout gumboots and jump on the back of the truck – there's a long day ahead.

Tomato Picker

UNOFFICIAL JOB TITLE >> Ketchup Bitch
WAGES >> £3.00 per hour
HOURS >> 5 a.m. – 3 p.m. Monday to Saturday
UNIFORM >> Whatever you have no wish to wear in polite society again
SPECIALIST SKILLS >> Nimble fingers, no fear of insects and a
willingness to avoid tomato-based products in the diet

We eat a lot of tomatoes in this country. Not as many as the Spanish or
indeed the Italians, but a great deal nonetheless. We are not talking here
necessarily about the beefy succulent fruits you neatly slice into attractive
segments and decorate with your best attempts at vinaigrette, although
those do count, but the ones that cover your shrink-wrapped pizza from the
supermarket. The overripe red orbs that get pulverised into a thin sauce that
the local trattoria spreads over your cannelloni. The chunks that find a home
in your tub of Greek salad from the deli counter. The ones in your ketchup
and the ones in your purée. Some of them are grown in Israel or Italy, boiled
and canned or stuffed into tubes, ladled into big plastic tubs and flown here.
Others are packed into crates and driven across continents. And some
are grown here, right in lovely old England.

Of course, our climate doesn't quite pack the necessary solar punch
to raise the things properly. No Tuscan terraces and summers to ripen
them until they are fat and sweet with juice. To grow tomatoes in the UK
is a challenging business – one that requires thousands of pounds in outlay
to start with, and a huge greenhouse. Then there are the complicated
humidifiers and temperature regulators and heating systems and all
the other scientific stuff needed to maintain the crop at the optimum
temperature. Supermarkets and other efficiency-obsessed commercial

customers want regularity of supply: tomatoes that are the same size and weight and colour as each other. And the closer the better.

So it is in this giant temperature-controlled greenhouse that the tomato picker must work. Running along the floor of the greenhouse are twin radiator pipes that pass down the length of every huge row of plants. As well as keeping the tomato plants warm, they also serve as a handy set of rails for the pickers' trucks – which can be loaded up with freshly picked specimens and then easily transported to the end of the line for grading and packing and all that stuff. If this doesn't sound too bad, then heaven help the worker with a phobia of bees. They are everywhere, bouncing off the transparent plastic walls, landing on plants and workers, filling the atmosphere with fat yellow bodies and a constant low drone. And the pickers' hands are constantly covered in a strong-smelling green pesticide that takes hours to scrub off after the shift is over. The job is back-breakingly hard on the rest of the body, too – long shifts spent bending over to reach the tomatoes, constantly on your feet and, when not picking, pushing the large rail trucks piled high with their green cargo to the end of the line. All the tomatoes are green. There's no way to make them red in the colder British conditions and the heat from the greenhouse isn't the same as that from the sun. To remedy this, once picked, the toms are then stacked in big plastic storage vats filled with a special gas, which, while not improving the flavour one jot, does turn them the right colour of red that the consumer demands. It's enough to put you off pasta sauce for life.

Herb Farmer

UNOFFICIAL JOB TITLE >> Big Chopper
WAGES >> £3.00 per hour
HOURS >> 5.30 a.m. start
UNIFORM >> Goggles, rubber gloves, boots and a T-shirt over the mouth
SPECIALIST SKILLS >> Just be handy with a pitchfork

I Quit!

Behind every innocuous product that sits on the supermarket shelves is a manufacturing process of some kind, no matter how natural and wholesome the packaging makes it look. Every pub bore in the land has a tale about the horrors to be found lurking in pork-pie factories and sausage machines, but in this case we consider the more humble concept of camomile tea. Granted, we're not talking about the indignities that animal flesh must suffer before being processed into 'food', but the post of herb farmer come the camomile season is not one to be envied.

It's expensive stuff, camomile – worth about £1,500 a litre. So it's often grown as a handy sideline by farmers to supplement the breaks between the parsley and tarragon seasons. It's not the growing itself that's the unpleasant bit, but rather the method by which the crop is collected. Once it's grown to maturity, the plants are cut down and spread into rows where they can dry out. Then a large cylindrical trailer is attached to a tractor, and has many loose straps laid across its floor. The workers, features somewhat protected from the elements with goggles and stout boots, then stand in the trailer with their pitchforks at the ready.

As the tractor passes over the rows of dried plants, a mechanical scoop picks them up and places them on an elevated conveyor belt, which then drops them into the trailer. There the workers must spread them out over the

floor as evenly as possible. When the trailer is full, everyone gets out, binds the pressed bundle of plants with the straps and then off they go to fill up the trailer again. Now that doesn't sound too bad, does it? But consider it closely – workers have to spend all day on their feet with a mask and goggles on, with a mechanical device dropping an unending stream of dusty, scratchy plant matter over their heads.

There's also the other detritus to consider – the elevator that carries all the camomile plants is not a precise piece of equipment. So, along with the actual crops, there's also a constant stream of stones, dirt, mulch and other rubbish from the fields raining down on them. Bear in mind that the cutting machine that chopped the plants down in the first place is no laser-guided marvel either – birds, rabbits and other wildlife often fall victim to its blades and lay putrefying in the fields for a couple of weeks before being scooped up and dropped onto the heads of the unfortunate workers.

So that means that your nice cup of soothing night-time herbal tea has in all likelihood been trodden on by the boots of several minimum-wage workers, mixed with a bit of mud and some stones, and possibly even been the resting place of a few dozen dead birds and rabbits. Drink up!

CHAPTER FOUR

ANIMAL MAGIC

NOTHING TO BE DONE REALLY ABOUT ANIMALS. ANYTHING YOU DO LOOKS FOOLISH. THE ANSWER ISN'T IN US. IT'S ALMOST AS IF WE'RE PUT HERE ON EARTH TO SHOW HOW SILLY THEY AREN'T.   **RUSSELL HOBAN**

We have a strange relationship with animals. We can spend all day running about in the park with one, throwing sticks for it to fetch and buying it fancy food, then sit down at the dinner table and tuck into several well-cooked slices of another one. Some we keep in gilded cages while others live for only six weeks before ending up on restaurant tables. In Britain, we are often regarded as being some of the most ardent lovers of animals in the world, yet our consumption of meat continues to rise year after year.

Both the ones we think are cute and the ones we think are tasty have created vast industries dedicated to the raising, care, welfare, fattening and dispatch of animals in various forms. They all require workers to enter the court of the animal kingdom – although some show less respect than others. From zoos to meat factories, we examine the lot of the individuals who wrestle with various species to earn their daily crust.

UNOFFICIAL JOB TITLE >> Featherbrain
WAGES >> £0.80p for a cock, £1.50 for a hen
HOURS >> 6 a.m. – 6 p.m.
UNIFORM >> Rubber gloves, overalls, shoe covers and a hairnet
SPECIALIST SKILLS >> Quick fingers and indifference to suffering, death, blood, etc.

The unfortunate turkey has a permanent place in Western culinary culture. Despite its bland flavour and tendency to dryness, we eat millions of them every year in drumsticks, low-fat turkey slices and in that weird pink turkey/ham stuff. Turkey also takes pride of place at the Christmas dinner table, promoting paternal flatulence and sending everyone to sleep after eating it in front of *Only Fools and Horses*.

It's an inexpensive food. Pound for pound, it's one of the cheapest forms of animal protein available. So let's take a peek at how these sorry, wattle-necked, gobbling critters make it from the farm to the dinner table.

First they have to be herded up and funnelled into the factory, where the process of turning them from live birds into conveniently shaped nuggets begins. The easiest, cheapest and quickest way to kill them is by suspending them by their claws on a hook attached to a moving belt, which carries them along, head down, to where their necks are broken by hand. They are then ferried around on the line to another part of the factory where teams of pluckers remove the feathers.

As if the slaughter was not harrowing enough, this is the really difficult part. Turkeys, like their famous chicken brethren, tend to twitch violently even after they're dead, making the process of pulling their feathers out something of a challenge. There's a premium on the skin being intact –

workers get 50p less per bird if the skin is torn – so the pluckers have to be careful. Another hazard is the blood. When turkey necks are broken, the flesh is often torn and they bleed profusely. So, as the birds move down the line, rotating on their hooks and twitching in the general direction of the pluckers, their conveyance often leads to turkey blood spraying in all directions – hence the need for overalls and goggles. Every few days, a bloke comes in to power-hose the blood off the walls.

From hereon in there are a few more steps to get their innards cleaned out and faecal matter removed. Their heads and claws are chopped off and they are then bound up with string and shipped off to be eaten whole or cut up into portions and shrink-wrapped into plastic boxes ready for the supermarket shelves. Or they might be mashed into a pulp with a bunch of additives and flavouring agents before being breaded and fried and turned into the lunchtime favourite, the turkey escalope. You might not fancy being a plucker, but look on the bright side . . . the last person to complain ended up working the neck-breaking machine.

UNOFFICIAL JOB TITLE >> Chicken Shit Shoveller
WAGES >> £180.00 per week
HOURS >> Long, miserable and filled with self-loathing
UNIFORM >> Something you can hose down
SPECIALIST SKILLS >> To withstand working long hours caked in
excrement, an ability to ignore the plight of thousands of caged
and condemned animals, and a willingness to forever avoid
frozen chicken burgers

Many people might claim that they have to put up with a lot of crap in their day-to-day work, but few will come closer to the truth of that statement than the humble cleaner at the battery chicken farm. First, let us consider the lot of the chickens themselves. To maximise their market value and keep costs down, the beady-eyed blighters are packed together in massive, low-lit sheds by the thousand in tiny cages that are barely bigger than the birds themselves. Here they are rapidly fed low-grade food as fast as possible in order that they grow into plump, easily digestible fare for hungry shoppers.

In battery farms there are dozens of sheds, each filled with thousands of birds. In order to prevent disease, and for ease of access, the cages are several feet above the ground . . . which is where the cleaner comes in. Thousands of birds being constantly fed means thousands of chickens emptying their artificially swollen bellies at a prodigiously high volume. As health regulations require that they not sit around in their own filth for too long, the cleaner must toil vigilantly underneath these cages to stem the rising tide.

So, in a low-lit shed with nothing but countless unfortunate birds for company, the cleaner must don a protective plastic all-over suit to prevent any ammonia-filled, disease-ridden chicken waste from getting into their eyes or down their throats. They then must spend their entire working day

shovelling load after load of this stuff into plastic bins, take them outside, empty them into a huge cesspool and start again. And it's not as if the chickens have the kind of diet that keeps them regular, so, as the cleaners move around under the cages, they are constantly befouled as they work. You couldn't ask for a more graphic reminder of your status in the employment market.

Having a boring job is bad. Having a disgusting job is worse. Having one that's both is pretty unthinkable. But if you can imagine that the battery chicken is the absolute bottom of the food chain and one of the lowest-status animals on the planet, what it does to your self-esteem to know that you're spending your life beneath them does not bear thinking about.

UNOFFICIAL JOB TITLE >> Animal Lover

WAGES >> Unknown

HOURS >> 4 a.m. – noon six days a week

UNIFORM >> A pair of sturdy rubber gloves and several sets of clean overalls

SPECIALIST SKILLS >> A deeper love for animals than most people

I quit!

In order to preserve the income for zoos and provide a long line of healthy inhabitants for future gangs of schoolchildren to gawk at, several zoos in the UK run their own repositories of sperm and animal tissue in order to help preserve species. However, the animals themselves don't exactly queue up to donate, so the thankless task of collecting the sperm falls to their employees instead. Rounds begin at 4 a.m. 'We start so early in the morning because a lot of the animals have "morning glory" when they wake up, and it's easier to collect the sperm,' says a despondent employee whom we'll call Bill.

Wearing rubber gloves and carrying a cooler box filled with ice and plastic containers, Bill, 25, told us that he'd just graduated from a Northern university with a diploma in life sciences. He liked nature and animals, and thought that this particular zoo would be the perfect place to work. 'I never thought I'd be giving an orang-utan a hand job every morning,' he said somewhat ruefully. 'And he is the worst; he expects to be kissed first.'

Every week Bill is required to approach the orang-utan enclosure, where one of the most valued residents can be found, usually lying casually on his back, hands behind his head and sporting a huge erection. After applying the massage oil onto his gloves, Bill must linger outside the enclosure before entering and kneeling before the orange beast. It takes roughly two minutes

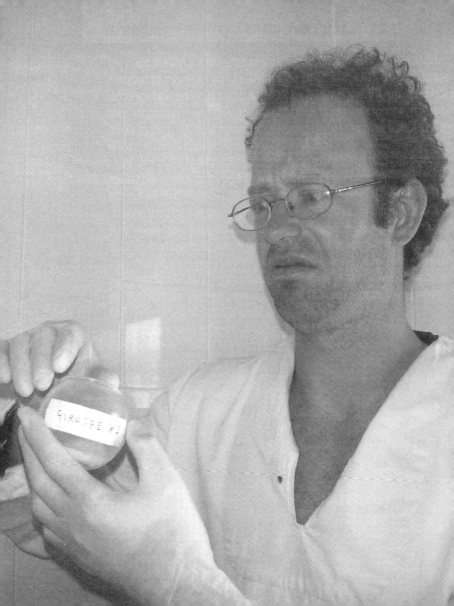

before the primate delivers the requisite sample volume, after which Bill must take care to leave the enclosure at the correct pace, ensuring his safety.

Next, Bill must enter the tiger enclosure, where the big cats sprawl lazily on the grass verges. Bill attempts levity in a somewhat half-hearted manner as he puts on a fresh set of gloves and enters the enclosure. Moments later, he emerges with several more containers full of viscous fluid. While many would see this job as an inherently dangerous one, Bill's visits are, perhaps unsurprisingly, highly anticipated by some of the more intelligent animals. 'They know I'm not there as an enemy,' he admits with a distant look in his eyes. Throughout the week he works his way round the zoo, finishing his peculiar duties at around 3 o'clock on a Friday afternoon after he's done with the tapirs, the rhinoceros, the giraffes and the gorillas, among others. According to Bill, 'Each animal is different. The chimpanzees are extremely affectionate and always enjoy a hug afterwards. The elephant is the trickiest because of the size of its member, and sometimes I have to use both my arms to get the thing to deliver. As you can expect it's really affecting my sex life. I can't help it. No matter how much I love my wife, on more than one occasion the sight of an ejaculating hippo has floated into my mind and put me off my stroke.' How long he will stay is difficult to predict, but the zoo's deputy assistant director thinks it is important to continue. 'It's because the animals have got used to Bill coming over every week to, er, help them out,' he says, 'that we'd be very reluctant to see him go. Many of them now can't be bothered to engage in real sex.'

CHAPTER FIVE

GOOD DAY AT THE OFFICE?

THE BRAIN IS A WONDERFUL ORGAN. IT STARTS WORKING THE MOMENT YOU GET UP IN THE MORNING AND DOES NOT STOP UNTIL YOU GET INTO THE OFFICE.　　　**ROBERT FROST**

The bland carpet, the uncomfortable chairs, the wacky soft toys on the desks; the coffee mugs with 'I Hate Mondays' slogans on them, the water-cooler and the wilting pot plants . . . it could only be one place: the office. Despite the massive variety of responsibilities carried out by people who work in offices the length and breadth of Britain, have you ever noticed how depressingly similar they all look? Sure, some employers try and fool you at reception with a plasma TV screen tuned to MTV, or a games console, or perhaps a daringly modern piece of art but, inside, you can bet that all the staff are engaged in the same joy-withering combination of monotonous bureaucracy, office politics, sneaked personal phone calls and idle daydreaming.

Here we take a look at the crushing mundanity of administrative work: the endless phone calls, the purloined biros and the time-stretchingly dull ways that business has invented to make our lives a misery. So put down that hastily grabbed sandwich and report to the boardroom for a company announcement right now. Reginald has got some exciting news about the office fancy-dress sports day . . .

I quit!

Customer Service Executive

UNOFFICIAL JOB TITLE >> Teleslave

WAGES >> £5.50 per hour

HOURS >> Six eight-hour shifts every week plus overtime, some night work

UNIFORM >> Standard office wear (even though you're on the phone)
and a fixed grin to avoid management suspicion

SPECIALIST SKILLS >> Good telephone manner, a strong bladder
and the ability to disguise the contempt for the general public
that inevitably develops

Call centres are big business. The modern demand for instant information
means that no company worth its salt would be without some form of
helpline or telephone support for its customers. Some industries are hugely
dependent on it to satisfy their customers, such as the transport network,
which has one of the UK's biggest call centres dealing with a variety of
enquiries. You can call the cheap-rate number at any time of day and be told
what time to catch your transport, where to catch it and what to do on the
way, plus how much it costs. All calls are answered by a human operator with
the information at their fingertips. Irritating as it may be to try and get anywhere
in the UK these days, spare a thought for the individuals whose job it is to
sit there like lab rats all day in tiny cubicles and dish the information out.

Now that some knowledge of the cell-centre environment has filtered
through to the general public, many people feel sympathy towards the
workers and attempt to be friendly and informal. These, apparently, are the
callers the workers truly hate. Targets need to be met and it's all about the
volume of calls that are processed, so, when the well-meaning chatterer is
on the line, precious seconds are being lost. As the rules don't allow for curt
dismissals, staff must watch their targets recede into the distance while
gritting their teeth and talking about the weather. 'Don't worry about being
nice to us – it just gets on our nerves,' says Richard, long-term call-centre

worker and delightful font of bitter cynicism regarding the general public. 'You might think you're helping but you're not. The best callers are the barkers – they bark their place of departure, bark their destination, you tell them the time and then they hang up without even saying goodbye – perfect.' Not that anyone should confuse this with rudeness, as the torrent of abuse the staff receive on a daily basis about everything from delayed services to invasion by alien forces would place a strain on anyone. 'It's always really bad after an accident,' continues Richard. 'After a bad train crash a couple of years ago, I had a female caller who told me what time she wanted to travel and where she was going, then asked me whether or not she was going to die. The temptation to say, "Well, I'll just check my database and see . . . and, oh dear, yes you are," was almost unbearable.'

Added to the strains of dealing with Joe Public are the Orwellian levels of surveillance most call-centre workers have to suffer. In a business where success in measured in thousands of calls, each second is precious to the company – certainly more precious than the dignity of its employees. They get ten minutes an hour of downtime, and that's for everything. Eating, visiting the toilet, taking some fresh air, everything. Nor can those breaks be stored up or moved around. Anyone taking too many unauthorised leaks can fully expect to be lectured by management on their bladder control. Their keyboards and handsets are linked to a central software program that records every keystroke, and the volume of calls they process, and allows management to listen in to their calls at any time without their knowledge, leaving everyone in a constant state of anxiety lest they slip up and the wrong ears get to hear it.

So, next time you're in a hurry and they've put you on hold, spare a thought for the underpaid and overworked call-centre staff who answer your call. You might really want to get to Reading on the 14.18, but at least you've got your freedom.

Insurance Payments Officer

UNOFFICIAL JOB TITLE >> Human Abacus
WAGES >> £5.00 per hour
HOURS >> 9 a.m. – 5p.m. Monday to Friday
UNIFORM >> The standard shirt and tie – wacky cartoon characters, musical print socks and shiny black shoes
SPECIALIST SKILLS >> A good head for figures

I Quit!

The business of insurance is a shifty one. As passive consumers we are constantly bombarded with advertising in various forms trying to persuade us to buy it. Not for nothing does the dramatic stereotype of the insurance salesman as shifty and of low social status persist in films and other popular culture. That said, business is booming. All over the land, millions of people pay monthly premiums to protect everything from the cars in their driveways to the Star Trek DVD collections that nestle on their shelves. And, to service this booming industry, whole hosts of subsidiary companies exist, lining up to take their sliver from your pound of flesh.

One such office rests in the gentle, bucolic hills of the English countryside. Here, to the gleaming glass towers of the business park, trudge hundreds of people every day, to perform the kinds of task you'd swear someone would have worked out how to computerise by now.

Here's the deal. IFAs, or Independent Financial Advisers, are not actually the Good Samaritans that the name would have you believe. They are actually just salesmen and women indirectly employed by the mortgage providers, insurance companies and other financial institutions whose products they sell. Every time an IFA sells an insurance policy, they do so on a commission basis, so, when your monthly premium for the insurance on your priceless koi carp collection is paid by you to your provider, a fixed

percentage of it is meant to go to the IFA who sold it to you. The percentages are tiny, and only become viable for IFAs when the income from thousands of separate premiums is rolling in.

This is a logistical nightmare, for both the IFA and the providers whose products they sell. Dozens of providers, different percentage rates, millions of tiny amounts owed all over the place. So this operation is a clearing house, a sum station, a big administrative calculator that can present each side with a statement of who owes what to whom and ensure prompt and accurate payment.

What this means for the lowly worker is this. A pile of computer printouts often up to a foot thick is deposited on a desk, which consists of several thousand minute amounts of money – 6p here, 38p there. All of it allocated from an insurance provider to various IFAs. The job? Check the amounts at the bottom of the statements are accurate. That's right – put every single tiny amount, by hand, into a giant desk calculator, and then pray to the gods that on Friday, when you've got to hand the thing back, you've done it right. Because, if you haven't, you'll have to start all over again. Kind of like a medieval monk writing a manuscript, but without any skill or beauty or coloured ink. Welcome to the wonderful world of the bottom rung of accounting.

My Story – 'I suffered media meltdown' by Wes Cracke (not his real name).

UNOFFICIAL JOB TITLE >> Media Whipping Boy

WAGES >> £60 per day

HOURS >> 10 a.m. – late. Monday to Friday

UNIFORM >> Low-slung jeans, square-rimmed glasses and hair gelled and sculpted to perfection

SPECIALIST SKILLS >> Fawning, lying and pretending you care about 'the brand'

I was deluded. I wanted a cool PR job – one that allowed me to do the maximum blagging on the phone, allowed the most mingling with celebrities, the most drinking of exotic free beers and involved a minimum of actual graft. When one company finally said yes to me I was made up. They represented some of the best brands; the office looked like a youth club and everyone, from the boss down, wore trainers and T-shirts. Add to this that the women who worked there were drop-dead gorgeous and you have a combination that is guaranteed to appeal to a twenty-something young blade around town who fancies his chances in the media circus. Finally, I thought, my youth-culture savvy and copy-writing skills would combine to world-beating effect.

For reasons unknown it was decided I knew a lot about online marketing, and I was assigned to work with their head of digital media. He was a public-school type who'd embraced recreational drugs like a long-lost brother and constantly babbled about the revenue-generating potential of the internet in a manner resembling Dennis Hopper in *Apocalypse Now*. The first time I met him, the word 'wanker' flashed neon in my brain, but I ignored my instincts, gave him the benefit of the doubt and took the job. How I wished I hadn't.

My downfall began one afternoon not long into the job when the MD flipped a pound coin in my direction, casually bellowing, 'Hey . . . pop and get me a cappuccino from down the road, will you?' Thinking that boldness was the way forward in such a progressive company, I replied immediately, jesting, 'Want me to do your fucking laundry as well?'

The room fell silent; the heads swivelled round. The MD was not smiling. It was downhill from thereon in. I couldn't do a thing right. Too scared of unemployment to mention I was completely at sea, my dodging, fudging, desperate attempts to generate revenue through IT gimmicks left me unable to sleep at night. My drug-dustbin manager then went on holiday, leaving me in charge of a huge account. The client had paid several million quid to make their launch the entertainment event of the year, a significant sum of which was dedicated to making their internet visions come true. I was wholly and completely frozen with fear. Every time the client's representative rang from abroad, my nervous stammer and avoidance of key issues added to the pressure. Something had to crack.

My most important pre-launch task was to send an email to a carefully compiled list of 5,000 'cool' people the company had on its database, with a clip of our client's forthcoming product to whet their appetites. Confident I could do this one thing, I accepted the provisional written copy I had received from another member of staff and, assuming it to be OK, attached the clip and sent it out.

Next day, I got a call from the client. 'What the fuck was in that email?' he quite rightly asked. 'This was only sent to me, yah, not to anyone else?' I knew then that things were going to get uglier before they would get better. Our client, in order to make a splash at the launch, had conducted top-secret head-hunting subterfuge to poach several high-profile products and people from a rival, whose parent company they depended on to actually see the project to completion. Delicate negotiations had been in place for weeks to ensure the parent company's nose wasn't pushed too far out of joint. And the email? Full of jokes that rubbed their face in the whole thing and mocked their now derisory range of products, several copies of which landed directly in the mailboxes of the parent company's staff. Total meltdown ensued. In a matter of minutes, I was hauled into an office and, when I explained the actions of the previous night, the MD's face went white. Two minutes later the client rang up and called him a c**t over the speakerphone. It was only the beginning. As word spread, colleagues began throwing troubled glances my way. I was a condemned man.

After a morning of running around, lying to the client and generally having his innards pulled out by a large team of the client's people, the MD summoned me from my banishment in a far corner of the office. 'It's like this,' he began. 'Because our client is in negotiations with XXXX, their whole launch depends on them. What you've done is damage that relationship beyond repair. If they lose this deal, they can't trade. It's our fault. Not only will we lose the contract, they can sue us for loss of earnings, and completely wipe out this business. In all the years I've run this place, no one has ever cocked anything up quite like this. Get out of the office and we'll call you in a few days.'

I never set foot in the place again. Amazing what the click of a mouse can do, isn't it?

Wes Cracke no longer works in PR.

Claims Investigator

UNOFFICIAL JOB TITLE >> Chin Rubber
WAGES >> £26,000 per year
HOURS >> 9 a.m – 5 p.m. normally, but may be required to travel
UNIFORM >> Shirt and tie, hardhat and wellies for some of the messier stuff
SPECIALIST SKILLS >> Little regard for the individuality in your fellow man

Insurance is not the nation's most treasured profession. Most of us regard the necessity of insurance as little more than the legal equivalent of two big blokes named Ron turning up at the front door and repeatedly asking if we can 'afford a fire' while carelessly flicking at a cigarette lighter. Whether we like it or not, however, the bullet of insurance is something that most of us have to bite. You can't buy a house, drive a car, employ workers or carry out countless other tasks legally without it, and you'll certainly rue the day you decided not to buy it when you break your leg halfway up a ski slope or your overflowing bath falls into the lap of Mrs Jackson in the flat downstairs.

So when disaster strikes, you dutifully call up the firm and inform them of the circumstances of your disaster. Your claim is then passed on to an investigator or loss adjuster, whose job ostensibly is to issue you with the necessary funds with which to replace your beloved fish tank, or fix the big hole in your roof or whatever. Their real job, however, is to root out all the liars and cheats who put up the prices of all our premiums every year.

Funny old business, insurance fraud. Normally respectable middle-class folk who normally wouldn't have enough of a criminal bent to boost a toffee from the pick-and-mix counter think nothing of padding their insurance claims with a few extra household goods after a burglary, turning their missing M&S evening wear into a designer wardrobe, pretending the dinner set came from

Harrods instead of BHS. It's seen as more of a cheeky misdemeanour than a crime by a lot of people, like taking pens from the office or claiming weekend petrol on the company account. No big deal.

All of which makes depressing work for the claims investigator. It's a bit like when people first qualify in the police force – they suddenly discover that everyone has something to hide, that minor dishonesty runs through all levels of society like letters in a stick of rock. Sometimes the claims are just plain cheeky, like the unemployed builder from Walsall who claimed that he'd had a plasma TV stolen. Not only was his flat so small that the TV he claimed was stolen would never have fitted into it, but the photo he sent in to prove his claim was of him standing next to the much-coveted TV in a branch of Dixon's, uniformed staff clearly visible in the background. Others are more sophisticated. There was a woman from the Home Counties who ran a chain of antique shops and was dishing out fake receipts to a network of friends who then claimed burglaries and split the value of the 'missing' antiques fifty -fifty.

Then there's the really awful stuff where people have lost everything and our claims adjuster has to walking around in smouldering ruins or flooded shop floors. Sometimes it feels good, knowing that they'll be taken care of by the money. But sometimes there are technicalities, clauses you have to explain that means there's nothing coming, no money to ease the burden. So that's a daily dose of theft, dishonesty, human suffering and misery, with two weeks holiday a year. Lovely.

UNOFFICIAL JOB TITLE >> Back Cracker
WAGES >> Pitifully low
HOURS >> As many as you can work
UNIFORM >> A nice but wholly unnecessary white coat
SPECIALIST SKILLS >> Superhuman tolerance of weakness,
whinging and poor hygiene

I Quit!

Being an osteopath sounds like a nice respectable career, doesn't it? Not quite a doctor, but certainly somewhere in that vicinity. You can imagine an osteopath's parents proudly discussing their offspring's employment status at a dinner party, discreetly snubbing those unfortunate guests whose children tried to be pop stars or went to art school. Helping people out and paying the mortgage at the same time, not rocking the boat too much. A nice gig.

Except for the fact that it's apparently a really horrible job. Firstly, there are the set-up costs. Dealing as they do with the general public in an intimate and deeply physical way, there's the insurance to begin with. Given the increasingly litigious nature of our society, it's mandatory for all osteopaths to adequately protect themselves against Mrs Melrose destroying the business because her back rub mysteriously turned into a fractured spine. Registration is another cost, as no one in their right mind wants an amateur messing about with their coccyx, and the professional bodies which one must be part of don't come cheap.

So, once these hurdles have been overcome and one can start welcoming the general public through the doors, the fun can really start. We asked Penelope, a former osteopath, for the nitty-gritty. 'You have to feign interest in the most boring subjects on the face of the earth, which

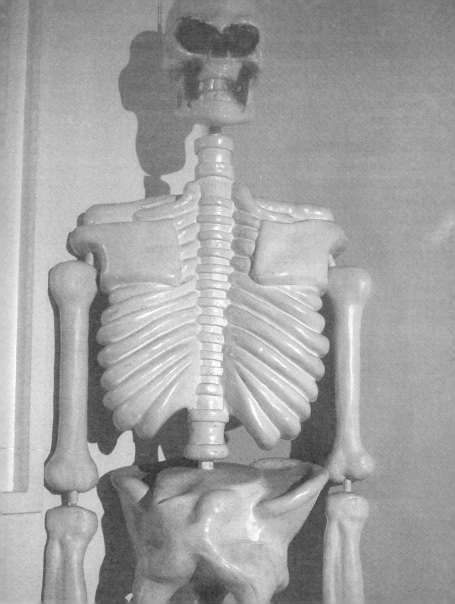

is other people's minor aches and pains. No one comes to see an osteopath for anything really serious and juicy, so it's incredibly mundane. Back ache, sore joints, tight neck muscles.'

Added to the constant flow of minor complaints is the issue of having to see a great many strangers not only removing their clothes but also expecting you to touch them. Questionable personal hygiene in one's clients is apparently just one of the more unpleasant aspects of the job. 'They tell you everything, these people,' complains Penelope. 'I don't see why me rubbing your poxy unwashed back for half-an-hour every week because you couldn't be bothered to get up from the television for fifteen years entitles you to tell me chapter and verse about your numerous infidelities or ingrown toenails, or why your children are such a disappointment to you. You wouldn't believe what people tell me.'

No matter what the skilled diagnosis of the qualified osteopath might be, all those who visit one apparently demand the same treatment. 'I can actually deal with a huge number of different complaints, from trapped nerves through to a programme to help people recover from major back surgery, but every person who walks in here expects to have their joints cracked.' Penelope warms to her theme. 'I can tell you right now that it makes absolutely no medical difference to your physical well-being whatsoever. They've all seen it on the telly, though, and just try and get one of them to leave without at least one pointless yet satisfying crack of the shoulder blades – impossible.'

Added to these pressures is the fact that, despite osteopathy being a specialist treatment that focuses on a small area of the body, customers who are too frightened to challenge their doctors have no problem laying into an osteopath for any perceived shortcomings, no matter what else they may have done to worsen the condition. So there's little or no intellectual challenge, terrible money, physical exertion, exposure to bodily weirdness and no sick pay, benefits, holiday or pension. Brilliant.

CHAPTER SIX

WOULD YOU LIKE TEARS WITH THAT?

SERVICE IS THE RENT THAT YOU PAY FOR ROOM ON THIS EARTH.   SHIRLEY CHISHOLM

Or it's the thing that makes you realise just how unpleasant your fellow man can be. Especially when six pints of lager have been poured down his gullet and he wants feeding. From corner shop to five-star hotel, there are thousands of service jobs that we take wholly for granted, barely pausing to give thought about who it is that's frothing our lattes, driving our buses or removing that unsightly wart. What about their lives? How do they feel? Would they like some cashback too?

Here we examine the world of those whose job it is to serve others, and dive headlong into the world of human indifference, cruelty and downright life-threatening danger.

Kebab Grill Man

UNOFFICIAL JOB TITLE >> Pisshead Target
WAGES >> £50 per shift
HOURS >> 6 p.m. – 2 a.m. Thursday to Sunday
UNIFORM >> White coat, permanent grimace
SPECIALIST SKILLS >> The thickest skin imaginable

Faisal and Ahmed have been running their kebab shop, or 'grill restaurant', as they like to call it, for ten years, since Faisal's uncle gave it all up and headed back to the family home in Istanbul. They do all the standard stuff that pissed-up Brits love to ram into their gobs come closing time: shish and doner kebabs, burgers, pizzas, fried chicken and chips. Their shop nestles unobtrusively in a grubby little parade of newsagents and carpet shops in what estate agents might describe as a well-heeled part of North London, where they can catch a lot of passing trade from the tube station and the handful of local pubs that serve the old Victorian terraces and council blocks that lean over the main road.

Weeknights are usually pretty good – they have a handful of regulars: a few students and mostly single guys who grab dinner on their way home from work to be washed down with a couple of lagers. Things get busier towards the weekend, though, especially when the pubs kick out. That's where they make most of their money, but it's also when the adrenaline levels really start to rise. Faisal keeps a big wooden club just under the counter at all times, but it's scant defence when things get really hairy. It's not exactly front-page news that a kebab shop gets a lot of drunken people in it on a Friday night, but the brothers have seen some stuff that would put most people off catering for the public for life.

'People can put up with so much pain when they're drunk, you wouldn't believe it,' says Faisal, shaking his head ruefully. 'One night, a couple of years ago, a guy came staggering in here, obviously very drunk, and ordered a large doner. We were busy and it was taking a bit of time to process his order, and he taps me on the shoulder and bellows to me to get on with it. I say we're going as fast as we can, so he says, "My taxi's outside and I need to get going," then he lifts up his baseball cap and there's a six-inch cut right across the top of his head. Turns out he's been glassed in the pub but wanted to get a kebab before he went to hospital.'

It's not just the night-time customers either, as the shop sees regular custom from local teenagers too. Despite knowing most of them by name, the brothers are still targets for the odd prank. 'Bonfire Night's always full of trouble,' says Ahmed. 'Last year we had a shop full of customers and this kid who I'd thrown out earlier for kicking my fruit machine came back and was hanging around outside with his mates. Before we knew what was going on, there was a huge explosion and our deep fat fryer caught fire – hot fat everywhere, burning napkins, people shouting and screaming. The kids had lit a string of firecrackers and thrown them through the door. We never did catch him, but I'd like to.'

Despite the dangers, the brothers are going to keep going. They hope to save enough to run a 'real restaurant' one day. Their skins are thick enough to put up with the insults and the shouting and they've survived plenty of aggro. Plus, they say with a little wink, 'There's a lot of drunken idiots don't notice what's in their food. No one leaves empty-handed if they're rude to us.' So next time you've had eight beers and fancy a shwarma, make sure you mind your manners.

My Story: I Was a Hamburger Flipper by 'Nasty' Nick Bateman – presenter and writer

In 1998 I was travelling in Australia and I ran out of money in Sydney, so I took a job at a local branch of a well-known burger chain. It was awful. I had to do everything – cooking burgers, fries, making milkshakes. The first thing is that it really stinks – after every shift I stank of fat and grease – it would take three showers to get it off. Then there were the customers. They either looked right through you as if you didn't exist or if they did acknowledge you it was to treat you really badly. They'd leave a real mess too. At the end of every shift I'd have to clean up half-eaten food from the floor, vomit, all sorts of crap. Behind the counter everything's covered in grease – the floor, the machines, the tools. I managed to stay long enough to join the '200 Club', which meant that I could flip 200 burgers an hour. The 'perks' included free food, if you could face it. If you worked less than four hours in one go you were only entitled to a small burger and fries, but if you worked longer you could have whatever you wanted. The only half-decent food I ever cooked was for myself. Needless to say, my employment didn't last long. I left as soon as I could and never went back.

Wholefood Supplies Delivery Person

UNOFFICIAL JOB TITLE >> Lentil Skivvy
WAGES >> £4.00 per hour
HOURS >> 8 a.m. – 7 p.m six days a week
UNIFORM >> Flimsy apron with wholesome logo
SPECIALIST SKILLS >> Ability to weave impossibly heavy steel trolley laden with food through shopping crowds

A certain small chain of wholefood cafes in London – certainly up until recently – used to have one driver/delivery person supplying all their outlets with huge plastic tubs of salad and soup and multiple trays of wholemeal pies, pizzas, etc. collected from the HQ and driven to all the outlets in a constant round of loading and unloading. I was that driver/delivery person. Fair enough that the foodstuffs themselves were of a higher calibre than the greasier fare handled by other unfortunate service-industry operatives in this book, but the logistics and deadlines of getting said materials to their destinations was tricky to say the least. Have you ever tried lifting and then walking with a huge plastic tub of boiling soup with an ill-fitting lid? Probably not. But be assured that the stuff will move. And scald. And land on something it shouldn't. The salads were a breeze. Carried the boxes on me head like an old-fashioned costermonger whistling a happy tune. But soup. Nah! Heat-resistant suits should have been issued as standard, but flimsy aprons were insisted upon so that staff did not look too 'industrial'. Secondly, it's all very well having the stuff loaded onto the van secure on its metal runners while ferrying it about in traffic, but try wheeling a 6ft-high metal trolley through Saturday shopping crowds at Covent Garden during the Christmas period and what novelty value you may have had of following in a long line of quaint, honest, be-aproned Dickensian workers swiftly fades.

Despite this, your language will be as colourful as a navvy on a double shift. The polite requests of 'excuse me' as you try to steer your way through hordes of browsers taking their sweet time soon turns into 'out the way, you fucking imbeciles'. There was also one small factor not taken into consideration by the head office. The route that I had to negotiate to the Covent Garden restaurant was cobbled. Soup in vats + cobbles + thousands of pedestrians = nightmare scenario. Mayhem in mushroom. Torpor in tomato and basil. And dumbass tourists covered in carrot and coriander.

UNOFFICIAL JOB TITLE >> Nosferatu
WAGES >> £4.00 per hour
HOURS >> 6.30 p.m. – 6.30 a.m. for four nights a week
UNIFORM >> Oliver Hardy hand-me-down blazer (one button),
stained clip-on tie, grey school-ish trousers
SPECIALIST SKILLS >> Stay awake all night with no mental stimulation.
To hold back the tears

The tie they found for me was stained and the uniform smelled of ashtray.
Then I was locked inside reception for the twelve-hour nightshift to guard a
block of luxury flats in West London. Above the security desk, eight television
screens showed black-and-white footage of the underground car park and
the front doors, from different angles. There was nothing else to watch
and books were banned.

But I was not alone: my colleague was old, drunk, smelled of an ape's
cage at the zoo on a hot day and only talked about horse racing, of which
I knew nothing. There was only one chair behind the desk. He slept in it
from 11.30 at night until 6.30 the following morning. While he snored and
mumbled about dream 'hosses' winning the Grand National, I stood up and
watched the security monitors. Or went on patrol – every hour – to walk
around a building that resembled the interior of the *Titanic*. Occasionally an
old, rude, unpleasant woman with a pathological contempt for uniformed
service-industry workers would appear and vent her spleen. But mostly I was
alone, walking all night, up and down six flights of stairs in two wings plus the
basement, to turn a key in a little electric clock on each floor, so the building
management company could be certain I was awake and not slacking.
Hallucinating through sleep deprivation, it began to feel like I was walking
through treacle as I removed sacks of garbage from the rubbish cupboards

outside the luxury apartments. They stank; it was hot up there. Most people die at four in the morning; by four in the morning I wanted to die.

At 6.30 I was relieved by a Polish sociopath who wanted to be top boy amongst the security guys and considered me a threat. When I went off duty, he would plant full rubbish bags back in the cupboards to get me in trouble with the management. About one hour after I fell into a coma of exhaustion back in my wretched bedsit, they would call me and demand an explanation for the garbage bags. Minutes after their phone call, television sets would erupt into life on the other side of the walls and ceiling. Doors would slam. The sound of flushing toilets and the inane cheerfulness of TV presenters' voices would keep me half awake until the next shift began.

I started talking to myself on buses. My sadness began to feel like the mumps. As time went on, nutters started to get into the building. The mother of a gypsy family once begged me for the keys to a flat. Another time, I buzzed an old, mad woman into the building, thinking she was a resident. She started doing a crazy Scottish dance in reception, kicking her legs high in the air. She smelled of wet dogs.

One night, the fire alarms went off in the early hours and dozens of millionaires in silk dressing gowns gathered around my desk and demanded I turn the alarms off. I didn't know how. The fire brigade showed up too, twice. Some of the residents checked into the hotel across the street. Only the Polish sociopath knew how to turn the alarms off. He knew the system was faulty but kept the information to himself. He turned up, grinning, at three in the morning to save the day. I considered staving his skull in with the torch. Just before I left the job, I discovered the electronic clocks in the hallways didn't work.

Lindsay Gordon

Genital Nurse

UNOFFICIAL JOB TITLE >> Knob-swabber
HOURS >> 1 p.m. – 8 p.m. Monday to Thursday
WAGES >> £18,000 per year
UNIFORM >> Stiff white coat, reassuring smile and literally
thousands of pairs of white gloves
SPECIALIST SKILLS >> Zero embarrassment, immunity to the
sight of male genitalia

These days, more people than ever before are having sex and they're having it at an increasingly younger age, when the words 'health advice' and 'sensible precautions' fall on deaf, hormonally confused and desperately horny ears. As such, sexually transmitted disease rates are at an all-time high, prompting all kinds of hand-wringing and embarrassing attempts to engage with youth audiences about sex.

All this means little to Deirdre, however. She's the veteran nurse at a London health centre and the phrase 'seen it all before' is perhaps more suited to her than anyone else. Each day when the clinic doors open, a steady stream of shuffling, awkward men come in, quietly praying that the receptionist is a bloke. Some get so nervous they start blubbering their symptoms to the receptionist right then and there, but she can usually calm them down before they actually whip anything out in the hallway.

First there's a consultation with the doctor – a quick chat about the patient's sexual history, a perfunctory examination of the genitals and that's about it. They come into Deirdre's cubicle for the main event, which is a full battery of tests for all the nasty things that can be picked up via one's old chap. There's gonorrhoea, chlamydia, genital warts and urethritis. Syphilis and pubic lice.

She starts with the blood taking, as it's the best way to approach the main event. It's a bit painful but not embarrassing, so it gives the men a chance to tough it out for a few minutes while she taps the veins and fills the vials. Sometimes they pass out – the big ones especially – or get really scared and lash out. She's caught a few bruises in the past when they freak out and run down the corridor, but they nearly always come back and apologise afterwards. After the blood, it's time to get down to the real business in hand.

In order to determine the sexual health of the male organ, a sample of material must be taken from the inside. That's right, inside. Even the bravest ones normally blanch at this point, as she has to unwrap two narrow steel cotton buds about eight inches long. Sometimes they're reassured when she explains that the whole thing doesn't go all the way in. Then there's the trouser-dropping question – when exactly are they supposed to do it? She realised years ago that a formal, crisp instruction was the best way, as some would walk in fully prepared, as it were, while others expected her to undo their buckles for them. As you might expect, some also get inappropriately excited by the procedure. It's mostly accidental, but security staff know the repeat offenders now and try to keep them out.

She explains that the insertion only stings a bit, but no one really reacts well when the cotton bud goes in, even less well when she rotates the thing. She tries to get the second one done as quickly as possible, but that one goes deeper. In Deirdre's view, things would be vastly improved if men knew a lot more about personal hygiene, but she's not judgemental. Having seen literally miles of strange penis flesh, there's nothing but professional medical interest occurring.

The final procedure is the urine sample, which the patients can take care of themselves. She has to be careful, though, as the pressure of the situation can get to some people. Having been forbidden to pee for the previous two hours, then rigorously probed, they sometimes pass out in the toilet and injure themselves, to say nothing of the mess. Sometimes she wishes she'd taken that dental-care option at nursing school, but mostly she just rolls up her sleeves and gets stuck in.

UNOFFICIAL JOB TITLE >> Verbal Punch-Bag

WAGES >> £18,000 per year

HOURS >> Six shifts a week

UNIFORM >> Peaked cap, shirt, trousers, jacket and sensible black shoes

SPECIALIST SKILLS >> Infinite patience, a keen nose for bullshit, faultless knowledge of London's transport system

I Quit!

The literary cliché that's always trotted out is that anyone who's tired of London is 'tired of life'. Well, Dr Johnson never had to man the ticket barrier at Leicester Square tube station when the Hippodrome kicks out, or deal with a train full of passengers at eight in the morning when someone's had a heart attack and the train has been pulled out of service.

Sadie genuinely loves London. Always has. But she can't afford to live anywhere near the centre of town on her LU salary. In fact, she's been in Bounds Green, right at the end of the Piccadilly Line, for most of her life. She loves the parks, the zoo and the smooth lines of Regent's Park, the pomp and ceremony in St James's Park, feeding the birds at the Serpentine. When she sees the lights of the Embankment from the top of a bus, passing over the river on a summer night, she's reminded of how beautiful London can be.

So why do all the people that live in it have to be such wankers? The reputation of Londoners as unfriendly might well have begun with a visitor's journey on the London Underground. It really does seem to bring out the worst side of human nature. Obviously things are a little more heated on the weekend nights, when people have been drinking, but it is not difficult to encounter the rude, surly, aggressive or abusive at any time of day. She's caught people doing all sorts of things they shouldn't in the stations – using it as a toilet, a bedroom, a shooting gallery. Most nights there's at least one drunken individual who has blundered his way to catch the last train and fallen asleep waiting for it, only to come raging back up the escalators shouting the odds, as if it's someone else's fault. Or there are the ones who barge into and rattle the shutters, screaming abuse because they're too late to make it home by tube. Many are good-natured, though – just high-spirited; maybe jumping the barriers or trying to run down the 'up' escalator.

The morning crowds are more of a handful. Pity anyone who gets in the way of a late commuter. The trains are impossibly crowded and hot; people are in a hurry and tempers regularly fray. Sadie is continually astounded by the arrogance of some passengers. One busy weekday morning at a Zone 1 station the commuters were crowding into all the available space on the carriages. They were uncomfortable, but mostly polite. Then, out of nowhere, a self-important balloon of a businessman comes bounding down the stairs to the platform, runs up to the open doors, which are clogged with people, and tries to force himself on the train. There are howls of protest from within the carriage and someone tells him to wait, that it's too full. So what does he do? Grabs this girl who is nearest the door and pulls her off the train, then crams himself in instead, sharp corners of his briefcase barging everyone out of the way. Unbelievable.

Women can be just as bad. It was a few years ago now, but Sadie remembers the time when a little boy, out with his mum for a day in Oxford Street, fell forward at the top of an escalator and got his little finger trapped between the floor and the moving steps. Absolutely awful – it took longer than it should have for someone to hit the emergency stop button. There he was, in agony, with his mum crying and trying to comfort him, the staff down the bottom diverting everyone onto the stairs, and station officers trying to prise his finger out. And, in the middle of all this mayhem, a well-dressed woman in her forties marches up to this poor little lad, slaps him full in the face and bellows, 'Why don't you stop screaming, you brat?' Then she walks off.

Sadie has her good days – helping the lost tourists, calming the confused, knowing that she's prevented serious injury or even death. But Londoners could do with learning some manners, all the same.

Kitchen Porter

UNOFFICIAL JOB TITLE >> Panhandler
WAGES >> £5.50 per hour
HOURS >> 6 p.m. – 12 p.m.
UNIFORM >> Hairnet, filthy T-shirt
SPECIALIST SKILLS >> Asbestos hands

In the annals of cooking history and the memoirs of famous chefs the position of kitchen porter is often referred to with a warm reverence, a kindly look back to the humble beginnings of so many careers. It's the lowest job in the kitchen hierarchy, the first step on the ladder towards Michelin stars, best-selling cookbooks and television series that entail living in the south of France for six months on Channel 4's money. Dishwashers are the lowly but honourable serfs with their eyes on the prize.

That's, of course, if you're one of the culinary aspirants who dreams of such dizzy heights. However, all around the country, there are kitchens where such wannabe chefs do not reside; where delicate dishes of the freshest vegetables and the finest meats are not being prepared. These are the chain restaurants, service stations, works canteens, hospitals and prisons, where the foot soldiers of public eating toil and conditions are harsh. It might not be the most rewarding job in the world, having pots and pans hurled at you by the latest superstar chef, but at least you're slowly learning how a proper kitchen runs. Chained to the sink washing up the greasy remnants of a thousand fried breakfasts for a conference of insurance salesmen in the basement of a Liverpool hotel offers no such heady dreams.

Kitchens are, by definition, extremely hot places. In the bigger industrial cooking environments, it's all about speed. You have multiple covers dining

at the same time and wanting their food immediately. The kitchen porter is at the thinnest end of the service wedge. He is not skilled enough to cook, but vital enough in the scheme of things to get bellowed at when things back up. He or she must spend every minute of their shift with their hands plunged into scalding hot water, scraping away half-chewed food, cigarette butts, ketchup smears and torn napkins into bins, scrubbing away at stubborn deposits of burnt cheese, swilling coffee grinds and pulling spaghetti strings out of the plughole.

Everybody hates you, of course. The kitchen staff hate you because they reached for their Bain Marie in the middle of the busy shift and it was still draining on your sideboard. The waiters hate you because, every time they brush past with groaning trays of coffee in their smart white uniforms, hot water and grease splashes out of your sink. The manager hates you because he can't understand why you can't clean every pan in the place, haul twenty pounds of spuds from the lock-up and clean everyone's work wear in ten minutes whilst making him a coffee.

Every two seconds requires ducking, as a red-hot pan flies into your sink from the hand of an overworked chef. At the end of service, when the owners are having a brandy at the bar and the chefs are all heading off down the local pub for a pint, you're still looking at mounds of coffee cups and a floor littered with the debris of a night's cooking, which must be left sparkling before you limp home, damp with sweat, skin peeling off your fingers from the chemicals in the dishwater and stinking like a cross between a burger stand and a public convenience.

All around the country, as the hungry hordes take their seats for another grey and tasteless canteen lunch, dreaming of the day when they'll be able to eat fresh lobster on the shore of the Caribbean, try to spare a thought for the humble wage slave toiling in the hot basement kitchen. You might not like the taste of your tuna casserole, but you'd like it even less if you had to scrape it off a thousand hot plates for a fiver an hour.

Roadside Assistance Rep

UNOFFICIAL JOB TITLE >> Michelin Man
WAGES >> £13,500 per year, plus commission
HOURS >> Various shifts, plus travelling time
UNIFORM >> Peaked hat, shirt and company tie, company jacket
and gloves for the winter
SPECIALIST SKILLS >> Pleasant manner, resistant to cold weather

Why wouldn't people want roadside assistance? You'd think that all the sales reps, families, businessmen and other travellers who troop in and out of the service stations day in day out spending a fortune on overpriced meals from the carvery and stuffing themselves with pasties might have time to spare a thought for what happens when they break down, but no.

Welcome to the world of the roadside assistance seller. You've seen them out there with their little stalls in all weathers, maybe a company van if they're lucky, or working one of the bigger service stations. The routine stretches out all over the country – from South Mimms to the far-flung corners of Scotland. One unlucky sod just gets to go round and round the M25 all year.

If Bob had one message at all, if there was anything he would like to share with the general public, it's that he has absolutely no idea how to fix a car. No clue. He can't blame them for asking, obviously, but it does get annoying. Especially when, after he patiently explains that he's just there to sell the service and that they can join right now for a special discount rate, they just tell him to get lost. Maybe if they didn't have to wait several days before they could actually call someone out he'd have a bit more luck. Or if he'd actually bothered to sign up for the training he could be out there helping people, rather than standing about in the cold trying to look cheerful.

The diet's beginning to get to him too. It's hard to resist the burgers and the pies, even if he didn't have a bit of a craving for them. Face it: there aren't many places to get a decent salad next to a motorway. He's got to know a few of the staff over the years and they give him discounts here and there, but it's no good for the waistline, no good at all. He doesn't like to think how many cans of Coke and chocolate bars he's gone through.

He was reflecting the other day how many miles he's driven and it was frightening – maybe 900 a week, fifty weeks a year. That's about enough to go around the entire globe twice over every year for the past four years. Bob's never been further than the Costa Brava himself, but sometimes, when he's standing alone in the rain, he wonders about where he might have ended up.

There's a lot of rudeness to put up with, too – people in a hurry, in trouble with their bosses or trying to control a mob of over stimulated kids. Often they don't have the time to be polite. Then there are the coach parties, with their mobs of teenagers and drunken football fans, trying to get round the back of the tent or looking for a cash box. He doesn't carry much cash on the stall, but it doesn't stop some people from having a go. He took a tyre iron to the back of the head a few years ago, but thankfully someone saw it on the security cameras and got them before they drove off.

You've got to watch how you carry yourself too – the inspectors from head office have a nasty habit of dropping by unexpectedly to make sure that you're 'representing the brand' properly. He's not slovenly, but it'd be just his luck to get caught out sinking his teeth into a sarnie, or sharing a quick cigarette with the bloke from the opposition. Instant dismissal, that. So he keeps his hands out of his pockets, keeps a smile on his face, keeps handing out the leaflets. Keeps telling himself it could be worse.

Children's Entertainer

UNOFFICIAL JOB TITLE >> Human Punch Bag
WAGES >> £150.00 for two hours, larger parties negotiable
HOURS >> Nothing earlier than 2 p.m., nothing later than 10 p.m.
Weekends not a problem
UNIFORM >> Wig, oversized glasses, shoes, trousers and hat,
red nose, bow tie and tons of make-up
SPECIALIST SKILLS >> Juggling, magic tricks, party games,
cleaning vomit out of your clothes

It looks like fun, doesn't it? The oversized glasses, the bow tie, the giant baggy trousers and the comedy shoes? Only if you're some kind of sick freak. It might be a dodgy way to earn a living, full of indignities, but it should be an easy one, right? Put on a big green wig and a red nose, twist a few balloon animals, eat some jelly and ice cream then go home with cash in your pocket. What could be simpler? Sounds like a piece of (lovingly baked and specially decorated) cake.

Except, as everybody with small children knows in their heart of hearts, that all of them are little sods who would destroy the world if they could to get their own way. Tiny, knowing, evil little sods. You think they're happily playing Sleeping Lions, but no sooner have you turned your back to try and grab a quick cup of tea and a breather than one of them will be grabbing your hand puppet and whacking his sister across the head with it.

Joseph was a promising drama student ten years ago. He studied at Manchester University, the Alma Mater of such greats as Rik Mayall and Adrian Edmondson. In his final year, they staged a modern production of *Faust* with Joseph in the lead role, and it was brilliant. His crowning scene was the finale, where four extremely attractive young female cast members slowly unwound the sheets that had been wrapped around him and he fell to

his knees, naked. It went down a storm – he was the toast of the drama school for weeks and got more than his fair share of action.

Since then, however, it's not been going too well. He moved to London and started doing the rounds of agents, castings, photographs and all the other stuff that struggling actors have to do. He waited tables, pulled pints, sold windows over the telephone. The struggle, however, proved a bit too much. The constant disappointment, the rejection and the false hope got to a point where he couldn't face it any more. So he started with the clowning. He used to do it for beer money at university with pals – a bit of juggling, some horseplay with planks and buckets, that kind of thing. So he paid a mate to teach him how to twist balloon animals and do a few magic tricks, borrowed a large sum from his parents and made some investments – the clothes, the wigs, a van with his logo on the side, some business cards and leaflets for the parents. He did one gig for a friend of a friend's daughter's birthday and he was off.

Some days it's not all bad, especially if there are a few single mums about. Often they'll pack the kids off home and invite him to stay for a couple of beers. Other days it's an absolute nightmare. People just don't discipline their kids any more. They climb all over him, whack him with whatever they can find, even swear at him, while the parents just stand there, or hide in the back room with a bottle of wine. It's not as if you can clip them round the ear, either. It takes a long time to learn the sleight of hand necessary for the tricks with soft toys and rubber balls, but what's the point when the birthday boy just sits there wailing his eyes out and covered in mucus because he doesn't like his presents?

It's exhausting too – Joseph's business cards promise all kinds of games and exercise as well as the clown show, because the parents want them tired out at the end of the day. So there are ball games, running games, hoops and blind man's buff. Nothing fun about that when you're fourteen stone and wearing giant trousers with a plastic hoop and braces. He has nightmares about keeling over in front of a gang of four-year-olds, clutching his chest as the wig slips off.

He always promised himself that he'd be a performer, whatever it took. Sometimes, when he's wiping the cake of his glasses for the fourth time that day, it feels like a high price to pay.

UNOFFICIAL JOB TITLE >> Jizzmopper
WAGES >> £6.00 per hour
HOURS >> 2 p.m. – midnight, six days a week
UNIFORM >> Overalls, face-mask and heavy-duty gloves
SPECIALIST SKILLS >> Indifference to scantily clad women,
strong stomach and liberal outlook on sex

Every British city has an area associated with sleaze. The number of sex shops, strip clubs and peepshows is on the rise despite the efforts of media companies, restaurants and local authorities who have all done their bit to make such areas more presentable. Man's urge to pay vastly over the odds for the privilege of watching ropey old strippers while drinking weak champagne still thrives, however, and several establishments continue to pluck greedily at the wallets of naïve businessmen and awkward teenage boys.

The peepshow offers arguably the most honest erotic experience. Customers pay for a private booth, one of many arranged around a central stage, occupied by a single dancer, who gyrates around in a faux-suggestive manner. The booth is hired out for relatively short periods of time – just long enough for the customers to reach their intended goal in privacy and comfort. As you can probably imagine, it's not the nicest environment to work as a cleaner.

The punters are separated from the dancer by a one-way glass partition – they can see her but she can't see them – a feature for which all the dancers must be eternally grateful. Every time the booth is vacated, the unfortunate cleaner must go in and wipe down the glass before the next customer arrives, as there's nothing quite so off-putting as somebody

else's deposit. 'We provide all the booths with plenty of tissues,' says one jaded-sounding manager, 'but for some reason they always seems to want to spray it all over the glass instead.' Given that the clientele are not always from the upper end of the social spectrum, sometimes they leave a great deal more than evidence of their love. It's not uncommon for the cleaner to find vomit, urine and faeces in the booths, as well as half-eaten food, beer cans, spliff ends and even the odd comatose junkie seeking a bit of privacy in which to inject. Once in a while they even get a dead body, as high-cholesterol punters tug themselves into a coronary-inducing frenzy.

You might suppose that the job, while deeply unpleasant, at least allows the cleaner to spend all day looking at half-naked women, but the appeal soon wears off. 'After you've seen them come dashing into work with no make-up, wearing scraggy old tracksuit bottoms and a top with baby sick on it, it's hard to get that excited,' moans one cleaner. 'It was quite a thrill for the first couple of days, but I'm completely used to it now. And, when you see the kind of guys that come in here, it's enough to put you off that kind of thing for good.' Never has the phrase 'I work with a bunch of absolute tossers' seemed so depressingly apt.

My Story: I Was a Celebrity Greeter by Andrew Collins – writer and broadcaster

My first thought was to reminisce about my first job, stacking shelves in Sainsbury's to help pay for a second-hand drum kit while in the lower sixth, 1981. It was, in retrospect, no worse than any other Saturday job but, because it was my maiden experience of real, paid hard work, it was a culture shock. Actually stacking shelves was fine – you just wheeled a metal trolley laden by older men with 'groceries' (tins of macaroni cheese and endless cardboard palettes of jam) out of the back room and into what was then called the 'shop' but is now, regrettably, called the 'store', whipped out your deadly sharp box-opening tool and methodically loaded these items in the right gap. As long as a customer didn't spoil it by asking where the salad cream was, you could while away solitary hours doing this until lunch, spurred on by the satisfying notion that you were getting £1.21 for each hour. The detail I dreaded – and the one I was put down for most often – was trolleys. This involved going up and down in the service lifts all day retrieving shopping trolleys from the carbon monoxide-choked multi-storey and beyond, donkey work lent a piquant twist of misery by the uniform: brown overall, brown clip-on tie and brown flares. Not an outfit to be seen dead in during the New Romantic era by anyone 'outside'. That said, at least to a degree you were your own boss; something of a cowboy, roaming as far as the Mayor Hold Car Park in search of stray metal steers.

But this was not the worst job I ever had. It was a useful life-lesson; it made if not a man then certainly a slightly hardened teenager of me. In fact, you have to spool forwards over 25 years to arrive at my real vocational nadir. This will, I suspect, be harder to pass off, as it involves celebrity and glamour. I was fortuitous enough to be attached to *Empire* magazine the year they launched their annual awards ceremony – the entire cast of

Trainspotting turned up, plus Damon Albarn, and Richard Griffiths accepted an award for *Withnail and I*; it was a right, royal, Britpop-flavoured rave-up. However, this meant that I was kindly asked back every year after that as an ambassador for the magazine, to 'meet and greet' an allotted star as they rolled out of their limo.

Being a 'greeter' is the worst job in the world. Yes, you get to shake hands and drink in the aura of real stars, but once you are assigned a 'greetee' your job is not only to escort them past the popping flashbulbs through the hotel to the holding area (you're a high-class escort!), but also to furnish them with drinks and 'make sure they're happy'. This is fine if, as has been the case down the years, you are assigned the charming Dougray Scott or the easy-going Jarvis Cocker. But not if your charge happens to be a serious-minded well-known British film director/producer, who treated me like a cross between a butler, a stalker and a mild astringent. Instead of being grateful for the personal service offered to much more famous people than him, he did everything in his power to avoid looking at me as we wound our way down the stairs past the logos of our sponsors, at one stage actually trying to shake me off as if I were an autograph-hunter and not a former editor of the UK's biggest movie magazine (I had a clip-on laminated pass and everything!). He conveyed, through a series of primitive grunts, that he clearly didn't need any help finding his table number, and when I procured him a glass of champagne he didn't even thank me. This is the best method I know of making you feel like hotel staff without the dignity of even the minimum wage.

'Do you need anything else?' I asked the esteemed gent, who had by now turned his back on me.

Primitive grunt.

I took that as a no-thank-you-very-much and made my escape into the throng, metaphorically throwing down my laminate like Clint Eastwood and his police badge in *Dirty Harry*. I vowed never to greet celebrities ever again.

The following year my charge was an American movie director and animator, often thought to be 'wacky' and 'fun'. I had once interviewed him by phone. This would be different, I reasoned. Yet he was even grumpier than the producer, looking over my shoulder the whole time in the hope that a passing tramp might give him an excuse to get away from me. 'I don't want to do this,' I felt like screaming in his face, 'but it's my job!'

The year after that, at the Q Awards, I was assigned two famous brothers. I was optimistic that this would go well, having met them on many occasions during their rise to the top. The older one pointedly ignored me as I formally reintroduced myself, walked straight ahead as if I wasn't there and as good as asked his minder to eject me from the hotel if I attempted to enter his airspace ever again. Confidence eroded, ego deflated, goodwill drained from me like the pus from a boil. That really was my last day as a greeter. Let them greet themselves. I was off to look for shopping trolleys.

UNOFFICIAL JOB TITLE >> Public Servant
WAGES >> £6.00 per hour if you're lucky
HOURS >> Varies from job to job, but long and hard
UNIFORM >> Varies from job to job, but good shoes essential
SPECIALIST SKILLS >> High rudeness-resistance essential,
as are deft hands and strong feet

Every now and again, a journalist short of a good idea proposes a story to their editor whereby a waiter or waitress in a busy restaurant attaches a pedometer to their ankles to test how far they actually walk in the course of a working day, with the inevitable conclusion that, hey, guess what? It's bloody miles.

Waiting staff are the stalwart troopers of the employment market. It's the traditional refuge of the 'resting' actor, the hard-up student, the newly arrived immigrant and the transient mover. No city, town or village is without some sort of establishment that will require the services of a waiter or waitress sooner or later.

The reason for this high turnover of staff and jobs is partly due to the temporary nature of the work, partly to do with the movements of the people that do it, but mainly to do with the fact that, in most places, it's a really hard, tiring job. People who come into restaurants and cafes are obeying an extremely primal urge, that of filling their stomachs, and, if you're waiting on them, their primary concern is not going to be for your welfare. You're just a barrier that has to be negotiated before the chow arrives and you had better not get it wrong.

As anyone who's served food to the public will readily attest, people talk to waiting staff with a degree of rudeness and complacency that would get them soundly horsewhipped in any other aspect of life. The clicking fingers, the beckoning hand, the absence of social graces and conversations conducted entirely without eye contact are daily occurrences for the average plate-slinger. Nothing is supposed to be too much trouble; no one can ever be too busy. The obnoxious and the loud, the gluttonous and the drunken, must all be treated with equal deference and respect. The customer is king, after all, and what restaurant owner worth his salt is going to defend an easily replaced waiter or waitress against a paying punter? Doesn't give out the right message to the public, does it?

On the Continent, the position of waiter is considered in more noble terms. Food, wine and the greater psychological esteem of being held in such high regard means that those who are its agents are venerated and respected for their skills and knowledge. Here, in Britain, it's a different story – we want our battered cod with chips and peas and we want it now, so the poor sod fetching it better get a bloody move on. If we don't have much respect for the food, how can we ever respect the waiter?

Don't expect much sympathy from the kitchen, either. Chefs are more likely to see waiting staff as necessary evils than trusted allies. A well-known restaurant manager tells a tale of managing an expensive London establishment whose chef had a reputation for his short temper. As the manager was seating some important American clients down for dinner, they were rudely interrupted by loud bellowing from behind a service door, which was then flung open by the fast-moving body of an unfortunate waiter. 'If you ever come back in here again I'll fucking kill you!' said the chef, brandishing a large knife. He then turned to the shocked Americans, open-mouthed at their table, and said in best Basil Fawlty intonation, 'Do enjoy your dinner, by the way.' From greasy spoon to three-star celebrity eateries, the waiting staff's lot is not a happy one.

Secondary School Teacher

UNOFFICIAL JOB TITLE >> Canon Fodder
WAGES >> £18,000 – £26,000 per year
HOURS >> 8 a.m. until 4 p.m. plus extras
UNIFORM >> Nothing flash, if you know what's good for you
SPECIALIST SKILLS >> A quick mind, even quicker eyes and a
superhuman belief in the goodness of young people. Eventually

Who in the name of Mrs McLusky would want to enter the hellish world of secondary-school education? I mean, really, who? Cast your mind back to when you were a teenager. Your mind is developing fast, as is your sense of self-awareness. Despite disgusting facial eruptions, uncertain hygiene and inability to deal with feelings of arousal towards the opposite sex, you are learning one crucial thing – that adults are fallible people. They are weak. They make mistakes. They can be hurt. More importantly, they can be hurt by you.

Teenagers direct a great deal of this new-found talent towards their parents, who, if they have any brains at all, spend their offspring's adolescence locked inside a steel box at the bottom of a well. But parents have to work, and they have powers to wield in their defence – the withholding of monies, the denial of night privileges and so forth. Plus, well, they're your mum and dad, aren't they? You probably love them somewhere deep down inside that moody heart.

Not so the humble secondary-school teacher, who is target numero uno for a whole army of teens freshly armed with barbs, gags, taunts and every other weapon they can find, with one goal in mind every single day of the school year: which one can we make cry? Besides the ignominy of being on a derisory salary and faced with a mountain of bureaucracy and marking a

121

mile high, teachers, far from being able to actually share some of the wisdom they've accumulated over the years, instead spend most of their working lives engaged in psychological warfare with some of the cruellest creatures on the planet.

Not everyone puts up with it, naturally. Every secondary school has at least one teacher with a reputation so fearsome that it permeates down to the primary schools of the town. Someone's name will be passed down by older siblings in hushed tones. One who brooks no insolence or horseplay of any kind. One whose lessons are conducted in an atmosphere of barely suppressed terror. One who metes out punishments like wardens issue tickets and whose assignments always, but always, arrive on time.

But imagine the sacrifices you have to make to get like that. How many drawing pins do you have to pick out of your arse? How many turds must need removing from your desk drawer before those idealistic teacher-training notions of social improvement and do-gooding are banished forever? Who wants to lie on their death-bed, look back and think, Well, at least I scared the shit out of some uppity kids.

It's no place for a sane adult. At least if you work in an office you can bury your head in some accounts if you have an off day. If you're feeling a bit peaky, surely the worst thing in the world must be 30 teenagers in an urban classroom looking for any reason to kick off. Maybe that's one of the reasons teenagers act up so much when they're at school. They subconsciously realise that anyone who wants to spend the majority of their waking week in their company must be asking for it. Consequently, they get stuck in with relish. Up the school!

CHAPTER SEVEN

STREET LIFE

DOWN THESE MEAN STREETS A MAN MUST GO WHO IS NOT HIMSELF MEAN, WHO IS NEITHER TARNISHED NOR AFRAID ... HE IS THE HERO, HE IS EVERYTHING. **RAYMOND CHANDLER**

They say freedom comes at a price – and believe me, the bill is a hefty one for not joining the ranks of office- or shop-bound. Whilst you might occasionally be lucky enough to feel the sun on your mush, take your shirt off in a heatwave or snatch a breather in a leafy arbour somewhere without your employer eyeballing your productivity levels, the nature of your outdoor employment usually involves close contact with something that no decent human being should have to expose their senses to – such as White Van Man. The pavement-pounders, cycle couriers and street sweepers we canvassed had all had a brush with this particular specimen of masculinity, whose wit, charm and erudition are often the cause of a surge in cortisone levels as decent folk attempt to retain their dignity and their front teeth and go about the business of earning a living on the mean streets.

Yet even if your job means you get to stay on the pavement, you are most likely cleaning it, or dealing with the general public so, with that thought in mind, the concept of outdoor work doesn't seem so rosy. Oh, for the sanctuary of the photocopier!

Sanitation Supervisor

UNOFFICIAL JOB TITLE >> Fools Brush In
WAGES >> £9,000 – £12,000 per year
HOURS >> 38 per week – different shifts are available
UNIFORM >> Stout nylon trousers, stout nylon jacket and sturdy boots
SPECIALIST SKILLS >> Tolerance of grime. Reasonable fitness

I quit!

On the application form from the local council, it didn't ask for much in the way of qualifications, but it did mention that applicants 'should not be too squeamish'. They weren't kidding there. The old saying that everyone always seems to attribute to street cleaning is that 'you wouldn't believe what people throw away', as if the average street cleaner regularly stumbles across the proceeds of the Brinks Mat robbery, or a fully working convertible Mercedes abandoned in a skip. The reality is that you would believe what people throw away very easily. All the detritus of modern life is there for the street cleaner to sift through: mounds of cardboard cups from the innumerable coffee shops that blight every high street; half-eaten takeaway food and its containers; plastic bags full of dog doings; used nappies – all the nasty stuff that you can imagine, that people thoughtlessly plough their way through in the course of an average day. One street cleaner told me of finding a crate full of tin cans stacked up beside the bins of a council estate . . . each one containing a human turd, but few residents were this creative.

You do get to see the city wake up, though. Starting at six gives you access to the curious subculture of the early workers – postmen, newspaper deliveries, bakers and grocers. See a few familiar faces every day, exchange a wave or two – it's certainly more civilised than the high street at midday, as the office workers surge from sandwich shop to bank queue in their hurried hour off.

Obviously the smell is pretty bad. Imagine the ominous tang that emanates from the bottom of your kitchen bin on a hot day when it's overdue for emptying, with that strange half-inch of rubbish juice that accumulates at the bottom, then try and multiply it by a thousand – you're not even close. Chances are your kitchen bin doesn't have vomit or dog dirt in it and isn't full of the day's waste from the fish market or the hot-dog stand. It takes a good hour to wash the smell away from a day's work and, to be honest, it never really gets out of the clothes.

It's exhausting too. On your feet for eight hours a day is one thing – lots of people do that, after all. But the street cleaner is on foot all day long with a heavy cart, a broom, a dustpan and all kinds of tools designed for extracting awkwardly shaped rubbish from drains and gutters. Sweeping the kerbs, heaving full bags of trash about, bending down to retrieve litter from the drain covers and scraping away at the chewing-gum deposits is no good for the back, or the lungs, for that matter. Working the parks is OK, but most days are spent right next to the main roads, inhaling exhaust fumes and dodging vans and scooters. It's a wonder more don't get knocked into oblivion every day.

You get to know the homeless people pretty well as they camp down in every warm doorway and sheltering tunnel. Sometimes the barrier between them and you doesn't feel that big. They're a lot friendlier than people imagine, although the council does sometimes order a clean-up, and forces cleaners to pull down the cardboard shelters and burn the blankets – which makes life tough for everyone, but it doesn't really change anything. They just come back the next day.

Then there's always the chance you'll stumble across something really horrendous – a severed hand or worse! There's supposed to be training for that kind of thing, but could you ever be really prepared? Street cleaners are always the first people to find the dead pets, medical waste and other horrors. Better keep those gloves on nice and tight.

UNOFFICIAL JOB TITLE >> Coupons Flogger
HOURS >> 11 a.m. – 11 p.m. six days a week
WAGES >> £3.00 – £6.00 per sale
UNIFORM >> Smart clothes for the girls, suit and tie for the boys. A concealed weapon might not be a bad idea, and some rubber-soled shoes for easy escape
SPECIALIST SKILLS >> Limitless reserves of enthusiasm, no soul and a love of chanting the company mantra

I quit!

There are many ways to prey upon the poor and the needy. The shameless hucksters of daytime television offer them cheap loans as a remedy to the big loans they've already got. Fast-food manufacturers and their high-street chains gang up to sell them cheap, fat-laden foods of dubious provenance. Other bodies encourage them to gamble on the lottery or the horses. The particular villains in this case knock on their doors offering them cards for restaurant discounts.

It sounds innocuous enough – who wouldn't want to pay less for a restaurant meal? However, anyone who turns up at your door with a scheme that involves you handing over £20 is unlikely to have your best interests at heart, and these cards are no exception. It's essentially a book of discount vouchers that might offer a complimentary bottle of wine if you spend over £50, or little extras like free side dishes or discounts for group bookings. They do offer a bit of money off your bill, but nothing special, and certainly nothing that would be worth your while unless you go back to the same place time and time again or regularly eat out with dozens of others. It's not as bad as pretending to be the gasman and rifling through the jewellery box, but it's hardly neighbourhood watch either.

As is so often the case with door-to-door sales, only a handful of people really make money. The chumps who sign up to sell the things in people's faces certainly don't. Working purely on a commission basis, sellers make £6 on every book of tickets sold, with the rest of the £14 going back to management. Before setting out on their rounds at 11 a.m., the sales teams are required to chant en masse before their bosses with positive mantras such as 'who wants to be a 9 – 5 cow' and 'I don't wanna be a fucking nobody, I wanna be fucking everybody'. They are also required to participate in 'pitching practice', where they hone their dodgy sales pitches on each other before facing the public.

It's a twelve-hour day, six days a week. Minibuses take the teams of sales people to various different areas around the West Midlands, where they spend all day knocking on doors to sell the cards. However, according to one former member of staff, the best customers are often cherry-picked off the list by management before the teams go out, so that salespeople often find their area has already been targeted. No sales means no money. Often they're sent to extremely inhospitable areas alone, late at night, with no idea of what they're going to get when the door opens. Threats and assaults are not uncommon – one former employee reported that she'd been invited into a house and kept for over two hours against her will, until the captor within realised she had even less money than them.

The only way to make it off the door teams is to be promoted to the position of trainer, where you get to drill everyone in sales pitches. As only the most successful sellers get promoted, desperate staff often resort to buying large quantities of cards themselves in order to impress their bosses. Those who are lucky enough to shift a few cards at the end of the day get to experience the privilege of ringing the big red bell in the sales office while colleagues chant ritually to celebrate their success.

So that's seventy-two hours a week walking the streets in all weathers, selling something that you don't like and doesn't work to people that don't want it and can't afford it. All for the possibility of being allowed to teach others to do the same, while those in charge relish the high turnover of staff and keep their monstrously high percentages for themselves. At least prostitutes make some people happy and get to wear exciting clothes.

UNOFFICIAL JOB TITLE >> Organ Donor

WAGES >> £2.50 per delivery

HOURS >> 8 a.m. – 6 p.m.

UNIFORM >> Bag, walkie-talkie, unnecessary cycle shoes, artfully customised bike

SPECIALIST SKILLS >> Little or no fear of death, excellent hearing, hatred of taxi drivers and accurate spatial awareness

I Quit!

Cycle couriers used to be seen as comic figures of fun. When the idea of bicycle deliveries was first imported from the US, the popular image of the lycra-clad and be-capped rider was seen as slightly effeminate – a job for the weak and the timid. Anyone who's spent any time navigating the streets of London, Manchester, Glasgow or any city large enough to support a courier business will no longer be labouring under that perception. Riding a bike on a city street is a hugely dangerous business. Cars, buses, vans, lorries, motorcycles and scooters all jostle with one another, trying to get just another six inches in front of whoever precedes them. The milk of human kindness runs pretty thin when it comes to other road users. Cycle couriers are, in the first instance, extremely difficult to see. Common sense would dictate that anyone cycling for a living should be wearing more in the way of bright safety equipment and padding than a ballerina playing American football. However, a bizarre mix of bravado and practicality leads to couriers eschewing helmets, reflectors, mirrors, front brakes and anything else that might weigh down the bike or make them look like wimps. And a significar number of them are clad totally in black. Consequently they spend every dodging past all manner of people who just don't know they are there –

casually opened car door, the unwitting left turn across traffic, the sense of impending doom as the bus drifts ever closer to the lorry with the hapless rider trapped in the decreasing space between.

That's just the other vehicles on the road. A lot of people don't realise what a hazard pedestrians can cause. Motorists don't normally have to pay too much attention to what's happening on the pavement; they necessarily assume that most sentient pedestrians have learned not to step out into the path of oncoming cars. Not so with the unfortunate couriers, as many of those jostling for footspace on a crowded street think nothing of stepping out into that small portion of the road occupied by fast bikes. Dodging the outswung arm of a rushed secretary or bellowing into the shocked ears of a gang of French exchange students is a daily routine for couriers. But the real animosity is reserved for cabbies. Since the dawn of time, cab drivers have reserved a special hatred for cycle couriers, by presuming that if anyone's going to take the brunt of their vitriol on the roads of our great cities it should be them. Woe betide the courier who nudges the back of a taxi or tries to cut across one at the lights – that's a quick way to the afterlife.

The principal complaint levelled against couriers is that they take almighty liberties with the traffic regulations – dodging through red lights, riding on the pavements, ignoring one-way signs and generally behaving as if all other road users and pedestrians are just so many slalom poles to be brushed past on their way to somewhere else. All this is true of course, but they're not showing off – they're just trying to pay the rent. Cycle delivery is piecework – they get paid per delivery. That's about £2.50 for each one. So to make a wage of, say, £250 per week (before tax) they have to deliver 100 items. Every second that their bag's empty they lose money, so they naturally go everywhere as fast as they can and take ridiculous risks in the process, such as filing down the width of their handlebars to better navigate the gaps between cars, or riding down steps to avoid busy junctions.

The one benefit? You get really fit. Most couriers do anything between 60 and 100 kilometres a day, six days a week. That's the equivalent of cycling from London to Brighton every day. So if you ever see one outside a sandwich shop, frantically scoffing an entire bunch of bananas in one go, you'll know why. And if you're ever tempted to clip one around the back of the head from the window of your van for cutting you up, give them a break – there's a whole £2.50 in that little bag they're carrying.

UNOFFICIAL JOB TITLE >> Carbon Monoxide Abacus
WAGES >> £6.00 per hour
HOURS >> Different shifts throughout the week, but five hours
at a stretch
UNIFORM >> High-visibility safety vest
SPECIALIST SKILLS >> Almost none at all. Being able to count
is a bonus, but not essential

I Quit!

The business of traffic management is not an easy one. The roads of our towns and cities in this small and overcrowded island are, as the press and environmental lobbies are always keen to remind us, nearly full to bursting. Balancing the flow of traffic in and out of town centres, protecting the safety of pedestrians, managing the delicate balance of traffic speed and the timing of traffic lights is a science. Many hours of dedicated undergraduate study go into the placement of roundabouts, the efficacy of speed bumps, the linking of camera systems and so on. The wages for those engaged at the top end of the business are considerable, as the economic lifeblood of many towns and cities is its car-bound citizens. Their traffic managers hold an awesome responsibility, preventing the nightmare of gridlock.

As with all skilled industries, there are those who toil a little further down the food chain, and the humble car counter is one such case. In order to feed their extensive studies and help shape their complex mathematical flow projections, the traffic managers must know how many cars are actually using the road. No doubt there are expensive and exciting computer systems that could do the job, but why bother with them when you can stick a foreign student or a pensioner next to the dual carriageway with a clicker instead?

This job is a particularly sadistic conflict for the poor brains unlucky enough to be engaged in it. No one in their right mind is capable of concentrating deeply on something as mundane as the passing traffic for five hours at a time. Yet – and here's the kicker – missing the count or being momentarily distracted defeats the point of the exercise. So counters must remain mentally alert and concentrate fully on one of the most boring sights in the world. Perhaps they get special assignments from time to time, like just counting all the red ones, or ignoring lorries, but the novelty value must wear off pretty quick.

Not to mention the pollution. Look at the window sills and brickwork around any remotely busy road junction. It's caked with the accumulated grime that's issued from millions of passing exhaust pipes, building up in a layer of gunk. On a hot day in central London, you can practically see the sun cooking up the pollution in the atmosphere into a smelly, almost visible soup. Now imagine spending a working week breathing all that in – not too lovely.

Then there's the physical danger. You might have a high-visibility safety vest on. But that's not going to be much defence against a badly driven lorry, drunken cyclist or some moron opening their car door without looking. All in all, it's a fairly unpleasant combination of extreme boredom and foul conditions with a high risk of serious injury. But at least they give you a cool little computer to count with, right?

Toilet Paper Salesman

UNOFFICIAL JOB TITLE >> Crack Wiper
WAGES >> £12,000 basic plus commission
HOURS >> 8 a.m. until whenever, Monday to Friday
UNIFORM >> Shirt and tie, smart shoes
SPECIALIST SKILLS >> An endless stream of acceptable toilet jokes,
willingness to listen to same from customers. An iron stomach
is also advised

Ian never pictured himself in the position of toilet paper salesman when he was at university in the West Midlands. Adrift in a haze of dope smoke and flowery English literature, he rather fancied himself a louche artistic type destined for a life of the company of gorgeous women and fiery writing, giving good salon and dying young and beautiful. That was three years ago, however, and the rent on his Birmingham bedsit didn't pay itself. Having painfully accepted that the market for gimlet-eyed writers in his local area was not exactly thriving, he decided to take the first job he saw that seemed reasonable. The ad only mentioned sales and a car, nothing specific. He only found out it was selling toilet paper when he'd agreed in principle to do the job and it seemed churlish to turn back. Besides, he needed the money.

The first day was absolutely awful. A phone call from the boss told him to meet his local sales manager in the car park of a local shopping centre at eight in the morning. After waiting for half an hour in the cold drizzle, a car pulled up next to his. A huge fat man with stains on his tie and bad breath got into the passenger seat, introduced himself as the local manager and said he'd just go off and get them both some breakfast. When he returned ten minutes later he presented Ian with a bag of chips. At eight thirty in the morning.

The job was, in principle, fairly simple. Load the car boot with samples and product, then head off to the local shops, garages, restaurants and pubs to try and flog the arse-rag of varying colours and thickness to whoever would take them. If they take a sample that's a start; if they take a box, even better, but the ultimate prize is a contract to supply them for a longer period of time – maybe even up to a year. It's tough going. No one likes unsolicited callers in their businesses and it's a difficult enough job to persuade most people that he's not some sort of petty criminal. There have been threats of violence and some nasty dogs to deal with, even before he gets to the uncomfortable question of what he's selling. At least if it was beer, or Scotch, or condoms, there might be an easy way to start the conversation, a nice joke to ease his way into the patter. But toilet paper seems to instantly switch people off. His employers are not the market leader by any stretch of the imagination, nor are they the cheapest. Even if he can get customers interested in the first place, it's not as if he can actively demonstrate how soft the stuff is, or invite them to give it a try.

His boss taught him a neat little trick – there's a clever little way of getting the roll back to normal after perforations in the sheets have slipped out of alignment, but it doesn't work as well on the customers as he'd hoped, and many is the time he's watched haplessly as sheaves of pink and apricot paper unfurl around their feet. The hours are long too – he often doesn't get home until eight or nine in the evening, exhausted from the constant need to be cheerful, the rejections and the endless stream of pasties and hamburgers that are the rep's staple diet.

Most of all, though, it's the low status of the business. He's grown up enough to realise that literary fame and fortune aren't waiting patiently around the corner, but toilet paper? He has to lie at parties now – he lamped someone after a few beers and one too many arse jokes the other week and it was embarrassing. He keeps his eyes on the *Guardian* Media pages every week, listens religiously to Radio 4 to keep his brain alive and silently, fervently prays that this is all just a blip.

UNOFFICIAL JOB TITLE >> Bailiff, Bastard, Homewrecker
WAGES >> £20,000 a year
HOURS >> Can start as early as 5 a.m. to catch the unwary
UNIFORM >> Shirt and tie, bomber jacket, nice stout boots.
Grim expression at all times
SPECIALIST SKILLS >> Quiet air of intimidation, remaining deaf
to the cries of small children and the tears of the desperate

I Quit!

Steven doesn't like taking people's stuff away. He really doesn't. But it's part of the job and it can't be avoided. A lot of people have got an image of bailiffs (it's a word he tries to avoid, but every single person he sees uses it, if they're feeling polite) as borderline criminals, thugs with ties who use violence and intimidation to get their way. It's not actually like that in real life but the prejudice is hard to avoid. There's no denying that he sometimes has to carry people's possessions out of their houses or drive away in their cars but it's a last resort.

They do everything at his firm – business debts, court debts, non-payment of fines, council tax, business rates, the lot. There's been a massive rise in business for the firm over the last few years, as the cost of borrowing and the huge marketing wave for loans directed at lower-income families rises. It's amazing that people don't realise what trouble they can get into, but he regularly sees households with an income of less than £15,000 with a Mercedes parked outside the house and a massive plasma TV in the front room. It's the shock on their faces that makes it so difficult – the rage at first, followed by belligerence, then the tears and recriminations as it all starts to swim into focus. Often the people who start off threatening him, swinging tyre irons about and screaming blue murder end up crying into their tea, asking for his advice.

It's hard for the borrowers, but at least they get to enjoy the goods for a while before they are taken back – no loss really. The really hard ones are the families, the small businesses – ordinary working people who've just let things run on a little too far. There's nothing worse than walking into a shop or a business and seeing all the hard work that's gone into it, the sweat and the hope, just to hammer in that final nail by loading all their stock into the van for the sake of a few hundred quid of the council's money.

Sometimes the excuses are hilarious – he's heard it all before. Been offered all kinds of things to forget about the debt and go away, if you get his drift. People hide, or try walking out of their houses with hats and false beards on, all sorts. He doesn't feel good about knowing how to suss them out though. He doesn't want to think of everyone else as having something to hide, a character flaw, a weakness of some kind – the work just exposes him to the poor and the desperate, the vulnerable and the stupid.

The moral arguments never used to lose him much sleep. After all, people should pay what they owe. He's always balanced his bills. Never borrowed what he couldn't afford to pay back. If he didn't go out and try and recover their televisions and their cars, someone else would do it instead, probably with a lot less sensitivity than he does. When they don't pay up, it's the rest of us that suffer – the honest and the solvent. But sometimes it just doesn't sit right, this constant battling against the inexorable forces on the downside of capitalism. Sometimes he just wants to help people instead.

UNOFFICIAL JOB TITLE >> Charity Mugger or 'Chugger'

WAGES >> £5.00 per hour

HOURS >> 8 a.m. – 4 p.m.

UNIFORM >> Casual clothes are fine, a different tabard every day

SPECIALIST SKILLS >> Super-cheery demeanour

A few years ago, it was something new, something fresh and quite exciting to do. When people realised that they weren't being asked for money straight away, they often relaxed a little bit, were more willing to chat. It gave the 'chuggers' a chance to really get into the routine, to explain what the charity was trying to do.

The trouble was, it was too successful. Once news of the amount people some of the street teams had been signing up had spread, all making monthly contributions via direct debit, everyone in the charity business, from animal welfare to medical research, wanted a piece of the action. Street teams began to spring up on every urban thoroughfare in major cities. With competition getting fiercer by the day, the boundaries between teams got smaller, with the result that pedestrians on longer streets often found themselves being accosted by several different charities within minutes of each other.

Ironically, for a charity initiative, all the street teams are paid and provided by independent companies who charge charities for their services. Many have made fortunes from the process. Those who sign up on the street do so on a direct-debit basis, pledging a few pounds a month which they invariably forget about, adding hundreds of pounds to the charity's coffers over the years without the contributor really noticing. It's all a clever ruse to

get around the fairly strict laws on collecting cash on the streets. By not asking for, and indeed refusing to accept, cash donations personally, the chugging companies can put large teams of people in key areas, unlike cash collectors who must apply for special licences.

Not that there's anything wrong with encouraging people to donate to charity, of course – it's a fine and noble pursuit. It's the rapid proliferation of the chuggers that has caused a public backlash, and it's what makes the job so unpleasant. Firstly, there's the basic principle that you're standing on the street all day, with all the attendant nutters that come along with it. You feel all the extremes of the weather – rain, blazing sunshine, sleet, whatever. Secondly, you're trying to stop passing pedestrians and engage them in conversation. While this might be an accepted, even encouraged pastime in more outgoing countries, in the UK it's a definite social no-no. We're a fairly insular bunch after all. Offer the average Briton the chance of even the smallest chat with a grinning stranger or a solid punch in the face and most will simply shut their eyes, stick out their chins and wait for the stinging to subside. They know what the chuggers want and they can see it in those eager eyes, even without recourse to the loud fluorescent jerkins chuggers are forced to wear.

Other professions stop people in the street, but at least they have advantages. Market researchers get to tempt their victims with free gifts or tastings. Muggers have fear and small weapons to help persuade people. Even the old codger with his Help the Aged tin wears the air of the enthusiastic amateur and elicits a degree of sympathy from the public. If you're a chugger, however, they've got your number. They know what you're after, they know you're getting paid to do it, and they know that enthusiastic speech about lame donkeys you've prepared will be replaced tomorrow with another one about global warming. They know you don't really care. So be prepared for a career spent watching people look at the ground, cross the street or develop a sudden interest in the screens of their mobiles. Prepare to be ignored for a living.

CHAPTER EIGHT

THE DOWNRIGHT HORRIBLE

THE RANKEST COMPOUND OF VILLAINOUS SMELLS THAT EVER OFFENDED NOSTRILS.   **THE MERCHANT OF VENICE**

I quit!

This is the bit where it gets really disgusting. Underneath the shiny floor of your nice clean bathroom, round the back of the gleaming high-street store and running under the feet of the beautiful people in their glitzy bars and hotels is the messy side of life. So that we may drift about in ignorance of the really gross by-products produced by humans and industry alike, unseen armies toil at the unpleasant end of the employment ladder – the bit that dips below the surface. They are in the sewers and the drains, the bins and the ditches. They get their hands (and sometimes a lot more besides) dirty so that we don't have to.

The following jobs are not pleasant, and you should be extremely thankful that you don't have to do them. Next time you start whinging because you've been forced to give the bottom of your kitchen bin a bit of scrub, take a minute to think of these guys . . . things could be so very much worse.

UNOFFICIAL JOB TITLE >> Offal Treader
WAGES >> £5.50 per hour
HOURS >> 30 per week
UNIFORM >> The stylish outdoor garments provided by major supermarket chains
SPECIALIST SKILLS >> Strong feet, a good sense of rhythm and a nose impervious to powerful odours

I quit!

The supermarket is a powerful force in most people's lives. Unless you're one of those hearty country types or were cursed with embarrassing, right-on, Fair Trade parents, the chances are you've been shopped for in the supermarket your entire life. Most of us visit a major chain at least once a week to feed ourselves, and they dominate the market for all our basic goods – bread, potatoes, milk and so on.

They also provide a handy prop for the teenage economy wherever there's a big store. While most other industries take the sensible precaution of avoiding other people's teenagers like the plague, supermarkets actively welcome them with open arms. They're cheap, they're happy to work part-time hours and, if they accidentally drink too much cider one Friday and forget to show up, then there's always another one who wants the £50 a week instead. Also, having their whole lives ahead of them means they don't view the stacking of shelves and pushing of multiple trolleys in quite such a depressing light as older workers might.

The earnest teen who ends up with this particular job, however, may get cynical a lot more quickly. Firstly, this job is located out the back of the store, away from all the shiny produce and gleaming promotional billboards that the public sees. All the staff fag-ends, bits of stray rubbish and other detritus that would put customers off is happily dumped here at the working end. This is

where the lorry loads of food and other goods are delivered, the cleaning materials stored. It's all harsh lights, concrete floors and no radio.

The job is basically this. Nearly everything that the supermarket sells is delivered in huge quantities – hundreds of boxes of cereal, thousands of tins of beans, eggs by the ton. Lorries pull up daily to unload these items so that the lowly stackers can get the goods on the shelf, but that's not where our man comes in. His job is to dispose of the hundreds of giant cardboard boxes that are left behind every day. To this end, the supermarket is equipped with a giant green compressing machine, essentially a big square box with a hydraulic lid, capable of compressing large quantities of waste into handily shaped cubes which can then be collected by another lorry and driven off somewhere else.

This machine needs an operator – someone to continually load the crusher with rubbish and make sure it doesn't get clogged. Which means spending most of an eight-hour shift climbing into the thing and stamping down on top of the garbage to make sure it fits the space before the compactor is turned on. Now this might just be plain dull if all you were doing was squashing cardboard all day – boring, but not wholly unpleasant. Until you factor in the butcher's waste. As they dismember their meat deliveries every day, the butchers remove kidneys, lungs, spleens and all manner of other animal bits that aren't meant for sale. It's bundled into plastic sacks and sent round the back for our poor treader to bung in along with everything else. So to the monotony of cardboard disposal is added the visceral thrill of squelching ankle-deep in a few sacks of random offal every hour. The smell is apparently something that stays with the treader for many, many years.

UNOFFICIAL JOB TITLE >> Meathead
WAGES >> £12,000 per year
HOURS >> Various shifts – plant open 24 hours
UNIFORM >> Steel mesh glove, white hat, hairnet, rubber boots, overalls, thin film of blood
SPECIALIST SKILLS >> A deft hand, a quick eye and nimble feet. Strong resistance to airborne pathogens is also recommended

Consider that less than two generations ago a portion of meat was something to be prized, a weekly treat to be looked forward to. Now, hardly a day goes by when most of us don't consume beef, chicken or pork in a dizzying array of products from burgers and hot dogs through to sandwich fillings and pizza toppings.

It all has to come from somewhere. As a result of our increased consumption, the raising of animals and their slaughter for the pot has grown faster, and more industrialised. The business of killing and butchering animals, once a highly skilled and remunerated profession, has been, in most part, replaced by machines.

However, a few people are still needed in the abattoir, and they had better be made of strong stuff. Apart from the grim reality of having to snuff out living creatures, there's blood everywhere that must be cleaned off the killing floor. The stomachs of cows, full of hot excrement from the intensive feeding process, must be cut open and drained, well away from the cutting tables. Other inedible parts such as spines must be stacked up and disposed of. It's smelly, dirty, slippery, dangerous work.

Abattoir workers are engaged in one of the most illness-prone activities outside of scientific research. They are at risk from contracting, among other things, anthrax, leptospirosis, brucellosis, variant Creutzfeldt-Jakob disease and contagious pustular dermatitis. Painful skin lesions, breathing problems and dizziness are just some of a huge range of symptoms they may develop. That's from just touching dead animals or breathing the air in the abattoir – way before anyone's even mentioned the huge sharp knives.

Obviously meat needs to be cut before it is fashioned into choice chunks and packaged into the sterile offerings that we happily purchase in the supermarket. In an abattoir, it must be cut very quickly because the production line moves so fast. Bones must be severed, and tricky bits of innards removed. So you're working on a dark, noisy, fast-moving production line where huge carcasses are swinging about, everyone's in a hurry and they're all wielding super-sharp knives. You're more at risk of losing a limb working in the meat industry than in any other.

Then there are the stress levels to consider. For example, the noise from the breaker machines in a boning room as they crunch up what's been removed and process them into meal is around 96db. If you had a house party that loud your neighbours would gang together and have you lynched. It's also extremely cold, as most meat plants are required to keep their product refrigerated before and after cutting. Some even freeze it right there on the premises for direct shipping. Cosy isn't the word.

So if you don't get gored by a terrified live animal snorting its last on the way in to the slaughter, manage to keep an even keel on the greasy wet floor, avoid accidentally cutting your arms off, being knocked over or crushed by a giant beef carcass, get frostbite from the chiller or contract a nasty disease from infected meat or go mad from the stress, you might just have a good working day. Good luck for tomorrow. Mine's a veggie burger, please, mate.

Sewage Safety Supervisor

UNOFFICIAL JOB TITLE >> Toxic Dipstick
WAGES >> £18,000 per year
HOURS >> Five seven-hour shifts a week
UNIFORM >> All-over chemical protection suit sealed at the ankles, wrists and neck, goggles and sealed face-mask, heavy sealed rubber gloves
SPECIALIST SKILLS >> A good sense of balance, no sense of smell and a willingness to avoid public contact after work

The most obvious thing is the smell – the people in the nearby houses complain about it all the time, but nothing can quite prepare you for the stench when you're working right next to the pits. Even with a gas mask, it's incredibly acrid and impossible to ignore. People think that after a few days or weeks it must go away, that you'd get used to it, but it doesn't happen that way. Some of the older workers claim to have lost their sense of smell altogether, but who would want that? Better to just knuckle down and get on with it. A set of clothes devoted to work is necessary, as the stench permeates into everything. You can't take off the protective suit and go down the pub, as no one will sit next to you.

Most sewage-treatment plants are called something else – water-processing facilities, public-health plants, something like that. But they all serve the same purpose. Whatever goes down the local toilets – and most plants deal with the effluent of on average 30,000 homes – ends up in a series of giant circular outdoor pits, each of which contains a huge rotating sluice to prevent a crust forming on the top. Sewage, however, is volatile stuff, and it isn't just left to decompose, as dangerous levels of methane and other gases can build up and cause problems for workers and nearby residents.

This is where the supervisor comes in. A huge array of probes, tubes, valves and other machinery is utilised within the tanks to add gases and

chemicals to the slurry, monitor the levels of bacteria and generally ensure that things are well. As you might imagine, most of these monitors have to be contained within the slurry itself and require constant supervision. So the daily routine of the supervisor consists of pulling tubes out of the pit, cleaning them off, checking levels, recording the results and starting all over again. The suit makes conversation difficult and it has to be worn all day because it takes so long to get in and out of. There's not much in the way of conversation anyway; everyone just wants to get the day over with and go home. Eating is also a problem, as the smell tends to make food difficult to appreciate. Most of the workers eat before work and late in the evening when they get home.

But the worst thing is what turns up in the pits themselves. People use their toilets to dispose of an alarming amount of things other than that for which it was intended. The staff have to be constantly vigilant for human organs and limbs, unwanted pets, packages of illegal drugs and anything else the unscrupulous choose to flush down the khazi. Most employees don't last more than a couple of years.

Sewage Safety Supervisor

Odour Judge

UNOFFICIAL JOB TITLE >> Fart Catcher
WAGES >> £18,500 per year
HOURS >> 9 a.m. – 5 p.m. Monday to Friday
UNIFORM >> White lab coat, rubber gloves and goggles
SPECIALIST SKILLS >> Sensitive nostrils and a great
sense of humour

The application of science to the methods of modern industrial production
has taken us down many an obscure road. In the quest to find better and
faster ways to make products fly off shelves, some of the best scientific
brains in the world have been hijacked in the service of capitalism. Instead of
trying to cure the common cold or devoting their time to inventing a car that
can run on water, scientists often take the money instead, and spend months
creating a super-concentrated bacon flavour for crisps, or trying to invent
a cheese slice that won't sweat when stored in a sandwich for three months.
Not for them the noble pursuits of Archimedes.

Nor for the humble odour judges. In the field of mouthwash production,
odour judges are a common sight – patiently sniffing at the mouths of foul-
breathed volunteers to test how well their latest batch is slaying the demons
of halitosis. However, in our particular case, these olfactory savants have
been employed in a far worse capacity. In a small laboratory outside of
Leicester, these humble servants of knowledge toil ceaselessly to assess
the effects that various internal gases have on gastrointestinal health. In
other words, they spend all day smelling other people's farts.

A small team of volunteers (whom, it can be safely assumed, concoct
untruths with as much skill as the odour judges when questioned about how
they earn a crust) spend the first half of the day consuming various quantities

of methane-inducing foodstuffs, then the afternoon with extremely undignified contraptions attached to their posteriors. Into these canisters rush the gaseous contents of their intestines. Then our lucky judges get to extract the gas with a syringe and place it into a small sample container.

When sufficient samples have been collected, the odour judges then amass their recording materials, blow their noses and get stuck into the serious business of inhaling the anal gases from hundreds of strangers. By rating each one on various different qualities, they can then build up a detailed picture of which goods create which effects, in what quantity they must be consumed to create them and, most importantly, which of the many gases that waft around in the intestines are most likely to be causes of illness and discomfort.

All important and significant work, you must agree. Not glamorous, not sexy – probably doesn't attract the big support grants or excite the scientific press, but it must take a great deal of dedication, skill and sublimation of Freudian hang-ups about the arse. It's difficult to imagine that there's much in the way of cheery office banter on sample day either – grim expressions all round.

You'd have to keep extremely quiet about your job too. One of the biggest complaints made by doctors about the social reactions to their profession is that, when they're off-duty and mention their job, people always demand on-the-spot diagnosis. In the context of the professional odour judge, it doesn't bear thinking about.

UNOFFICIAL JOB TITLE >> Toilet Brush
WAGES >> £200.00 per day
HOURS >> Four days on, four days off
UNIFORM >> Plenty of protective equipment
SPECIALIST SKILLS >> A distinct lack of imagination

I Quit!

The image of the commercial diver is quite a cool one: rugged, free-thinking individuals making good money by risking a little danger. Working for themselves, travelling the world, not tied down by all the regulations and petty annoyances that bedevil us normal working stiffs. For the most part, that may be true. But the working world of the commercial diver can take them into places that the rest of us would refuse to visit, no matter how much money was on offer.

Wherever there is deep liquid and machinery, commercial divers are needed. A lot of this work is where you might imagine it to be – oil rigs, docks, buildings that extend into lakes or the sea. There are rivets to be fixed, sheets of metal to be welded, poles to bolt onto bits of steel. It's possibly a bit cold and dark, but nothing too untoward. Perhaps we can even picture ourselves donning the equipment and plunging into the deep – it's quite cool.

Sewage diving, however, they are welcome to keep. Here's how it works. Most sewage-treatment plants have huge round vats called settling lagoons, into which the sewage flows from our drains. You've probably seen them from a passing car – big outdoor pools with gently circulating rotors to keep the surface from crusting over. All the mechanical parts of these lagoons are located at the bottom and, due to the prohibitive cost and logistical difficulties of emptying the thing, it's easier and cheaper to get a diver into it when repairs need to be made.

As you can imagine, this poses no small health risk for the diver. Firstly, they need injections for Hepatitis B, tetanus and cholera. Next, they must be completely covered in a dry suit (allows no liquid in, unlike a wetsuit), which has its own vulcanised rubber boots attached. Then rubber gloves are sealed over the wrists of the suit to prevent any leakage. The suit has a metal collar at the neck to which a helmet is attached. The whole thing is called a 'constant volume suit' because the diver breathes within the confines of the helmet rather than through a mouthpiece.

Then the lucky chap gets lowered into the settling lagoon. Apparently, the smell isn't as bad as you might think because the material is treated with chemicals to counter the odour. 'You do have to put what you're going into out of your mind if you can,' says Michael, who has dived into sewage twice. 'It's completely black under there, no light at all. And it's very different to water – much thicker and slower to move through. You can't see a thing so you have to work completely by touch. Often you haven't had time to familiarise yourself with the mechanical problem by sight above the surface, so repairs can take a while as the team above you takes you slowly through the procedure.'

When the work's finished and the diver gets to return to the surface, the next stage begins. Firstly, he is heavily hosed down to clean off the sewage. 'That can be extremely unpleasant,' says Michael. 'The suit makes you very hot in the open air, so you have to stand around covered in muck and sweating heavily while they hose you off. Then some lucky support workers get the unenviable task of removing the suit and all its parts so they can be taken away and sterilised before the next dive.

'The material is obviously not everyone's idea of a nice place to work,' says Michael. 'But the hardest part is the dark – you have to rely completely on your support team above the surface, because you can't make a move without them. I've dived in all sorts of other things – a huge vat of liquid cheese whey at a cheddar factory, for example, and even in a grain silo, but the sewage jobs are definitely the worst.' No shit.

Author
UNOFFICIAL JOB TITLE >> Hired Hack
WAGES >> I'm not telling you that
HOURS >> A lot more than the publisher said it would
UNIFORM >> Grubby dressing gown, worn throughout
SPECIALIST SKILLS >> Relaxed relationship with the truth, fondness for the limitless distractions of pornography, exceptional vagueness on questions of deadline

I Quit!

So, here we are at the end. I hope that you didn't get too bored and are certainly feeling a lot better about your lot than when you started reading this book. Since this is now over, you'll be able to find me on the sofa with a beer in one hand and my video-game controller in the other. Same place as I was before this whole fandango started and with the advance all spent on keeping the wolf from the door. Thanks for staying the distance, but really – haven't you got some work you should be doing?   **Tim Wild**

>> Neil Tenant, singer with the Pet Shop Boys, once had a job changing American spellings into English for Marvel comics.

>> Carol Decker from eighties rockers T'Pau worked as a butcher's apprentice.

>> Metal buffoon Ozzy Osbourne worked in an abattoir.

>> Soul legend Bill Withers made ends meet installing toilets on aeroplanes.

>> Country chanteuse Tammy Wynette is a former beautician.

>> The late Joe Strummer from the Clash and leopard-skin-wearing blonde-fancier Rod Stewart both once held jobs as grave diggers.

>> Johnny Cash sold vacuum cleaners door-to-door before his break as a singer.

>> High priestess and pope-baiter Sinead O'Connor used to make a living as a kissogram.

>> Elvis Costello was a computer programmer for a cosmetics company.

>> Cyndi Lauper used to promote wrestling matches to pay the bills.

>> Barry Manilow once earned a crust as the resident pianist in a New York bathhouse.